The Magician Who Kept a Pub and Other Stories

Here is a sparkling collection of traditional fairy stories with a difference: they all take place in our time. With her own special brand of magic and humour, Dorothy Edwards takes familiar characters – a witch, a giant, a magician for instance – and puts them in an ordinary, everyday situation. This, as you can imagine, has some startling and very funny results.

The Magician Who Kept A Pub

DOROTHY EDWARDS
Illustrated by Jill Bennett

YOUNG
LIONS

First published 1975 by Kestrel Books
First published in Young Lions 1981
Seventh impression July 1989

Young Lions is an imprint of
the Children's Division, part of
the Collins Publishing Group
8 Grafton Street, London W1X 3LA

Printed and bound in Great Britain by
William Collins Sons & Co. Ltd, Glasgow

For Emma Jane Brunt
with love

Contents

I

The Magician Who Kept
a Pub

THERE was once a Magician who kept a pub.
This pub stood in a market square in an English
country town. It was called The Golden Pig and
was famous throughout the land.

And why was it famous?

Wouldn't you expect it to be famous if it had
a Magician for a landlord? A Magician who
walked about all day with his coat open to show
off a waistcoat that was sewn all over with
diamonds and sapphires and emeralds? Why,
that waistcoat was so dazzling that when the
Magician stood outside his door enjoying the
morning sunshine it flashed and sparkled with
every twist and turn of him, filling the air with
the wildness of gypsy fiddles.

Then there was the sign that hung above the
public bar door. That was a famous thing in
itself. A swinging pig in solid gold – deep

red-gold, picked out all over in fiery rubies, so bright and flaming and daunting it was when the sun shone strong upon it that it throbbed and boomed like a great gong with vibrations that set the striped awnings over the market-stalls quivering until their colours seemed to run together.

And there was the Magician's daughter who was so beautiful it made you blink to look at her. She had hair as fine as spun moonlight that she brushed each morning leaning from her window high above The Golden Pig and as she brushed the lively strands fanned out across the brick-work and when she shook them loose it was like a waterfall – the rush and tinkle and splash of it!

Imagine the splendid glitter and flash and clash when the morning sun fell booming upon that red-gold pig and flashed and winked in the jewels of that twinkling waistcoat and ran sunbeams among the moonbeam tresses of the landlord's lovely daughter as she leaned brushing her rustling hair as it fell like a waterfall, cool in the sunlight. What a poetic sight! No wonder people came to stare!

On the other side of the square three brothers kept three market-stalls, which they set up every day and minded until evening came. Len, Les and Arnie they were called.

Len the eldest was the sharp one, the sly, keen brother. He sold fish, did Len. Every day he cried, 'Sprats and mackerel all a-fresh-o! Whelks, plaice and 'addocks still wet from the sea!

''Ere you are, lady, smell the salt if you don't believe me!' he'd say, sliding his crafty eyes.

The next brother Les, was the artful one, the lazy dodger. He sold fruit and vegetables: 'Apples a pound pears! Nothing wrong with my stuff. Don't mind the specks, lady – good for the complexion.

'What about this, sir – a pair of cauliflowers for the price of two? Thank you very much. Your change, guv.' That was Les.

That leaves Arnie. He was the youngest and the softest: the dreamer.

Arnie sold things made of wood. Chairs and tables, cupboards and butter-tubs – things he had made himself. Arnie never shouted his wares. He was the quiet brother, the one who sat and waited till his customers came, and was quite disappointed when they did as he was so attached to the things he had made.

And, of course, all three of them wanted to marry the pub-keeper's daughter – the Magician's child!

Fishmonger Len looked across each day and said, 'Cor – that weskit. It throws me. What a sparkler. Just think – every now and then he could pick off a bit of trimming and sell it for a little fortune. Oh, wouldn't I like to be that old geezer's son-in-law and come in for that weskit one day!'

Les said, 'When I think of that golden porker over there – solid gold and all those rubies – worth a bomb. Brother! I'd like to marry the Magician's daughter for the chance of one day being able to run my fingers through a heap of those red flashers.'

But Arnie, our hero, he would stand staring; seeing only the Magician's lovely daughter twirling and pinning and plaiting her moon-light tresses, and sighing to himself, would wonder what it would be like to pull out those hair-pins and let the soft hair flow forth again. 'Oh how beautiful she is,' he said.

At last Len, the first brother, took his courage in his hands and went across the market square and spoke to the Magician as he stood outside his pub looking up and down the street.

'You know me, guv,' said Len, in a sly and wheedling voice, his eyes fixed greedily on that jewelled waistcoat, 'I'm Scaly Len the fish-monger from over the square. Many a fat kipper

I've sent over for your breakfast and many a choice winkle I've boiled for your landlord-ship's tea.

'You have only got to look across the road to see that I do good business. It must be plain to you that I can support a missus. And, between you and me you'll never lack a shrimp for your tea as long as I can provide it – so how about considering me for a son-in-law?'

And all the time he spoke his gaze was on the waistcoat, and every word he spoke he said to it.

The Magician looked hard at Len for a moment, then he said, 'Well, that's easier said than done. For why? Well, I can't give my gal away to someone for nothing. Oh no!

'No. I've got a fancy. Just as you've got a fancy say – for my weskit – or my daughter, I've got a fancy to eat one of the rare silver eggs from the wishing-bird's nest for breakfast on my daughter's wedding day.

'If you could get me one of those, you can have my girl for your wife and everything else – I reckon I'd retire after eating a breakfast like that.' And he rolled his wicked eyes and grinned like the devil.

But Len whose own eyes were dazzled by the white and green and blue dance of that restless waistcoat did not notice the grin, he licked his lips in anticipation and said, 'It's as good as done, guv. Just tell me where I can find that silver egg in the wishing-bird's nest and it's yours for the boiling!'

The Magician grinned again, 'Do you know that high sky-scraping block of flats right at the edge of the town?'

Len said, 'You mean that very high one – the one that's so high its roof is lost in the clouds?'

'The highest in the world. That's right!' said the Magician pub-keeper. 'Well now, right up on the top there, above the cloud-line – up among the TV aerials, the wishing-bird has made her nest. And on it she sits, day and night, trying to hatch out her silver eggs.

'It wouldn't be difficult to slip your hand into her nest and take one of them – if she's so stupid as to think she can hatch out silver eggs, she'd be too stupid to notice a sly one like you.'

And he chuckled as he spoke and Len joined him with a snigger. 'It sounds easy as pie,' he said. 'Yes, I'll have a go.'

To himself he thought, 'What a fool this old Magician is – not to have tried to get one himself. And what a fool-and-a-half he is to talk of eating a silver egg that can't be hatched out!'

But, as he turned to go, the Magician who knew every single thought that had passed through his head, and was grinning like a demon, said softly, 'Wait wait, my dear young man! Surely you didn't think there'd be no conditions? Why, in situations like this there are always conditions!'

Len stopped and looked straight at the Magician, who met his gaze with a smile as mild as milk:

'There are lifts in that building of course – lifts from the cellars below the basement right to the roof above. But the condition is: THAT YOU DON'T USE THEM. The condition is that you use the stairs that climb alongside the lifts. You have to mount by those stairs. No lifts mind – and the other condition is that you keep a civil tongue in your head.'

As he spoke the waistcoat glowed like fairy-lamps to match the gentleness of his voice.

'Use the stairs – civil tongue. Right!' replied

Len. 'Any more? No? Then I'm off.' And off he ran, so eager to possess the Magician's waistcoat he didn't hear the rest of the Magician's words: ' – and no cheating when there is magic about. Cheating can be very, very dangerous.'

By then Len had reached the place where his little fish-van was parked behind the town hall. With a roar and a rush he was off. And in less than twelve minutes – so favourable were the traffic lights – green all the way – he arrived at the tall, tall building – the high block of flats. Looking up and up, he saw the white clouds clinging about the rooftop and concealing the highest storeys and below them rows of windows small as pin-pricks, twinkling in the sunshine so far up they were.

'Well, this is IT,' said Len the sharp brother, slamming his van door and locking it.

There was no one and nothing inside the great echoing entrance hall. Only a long row of lift-doors like gilded gates. As Len stepped towards them one glided open. But Len was too sharp for that.

'No no! Naughty, naughty,' he said, 'I'm for the staircase – like the gentleman said.' And passing the lifts he found the beginning of a stone staircase and began to climb, up and up to a landing and up and up again.

He had gone up three flights when he heard a strange sound – a scrubbing noise, and there, kneeling on the second step of the next flight, he found an old, old woman, with a great bucket of soapy water beside her, scrubbing away.

'Mind my step. Mind my step,' the old woman cried. 'Don't walk on it, it's wet!'

'All right, ma,' said sharp Len, keeping a civil tongue in his head, 'keep your wig on. I'll hop over it.'

And that's what he did, while the old woman muttered to herself. And on he went, on and on and up and up and then –

'No, not her again,' said Len. But there she was, the same old woman, scrubbing away.

'Mind out, don't tread on my step. It's clean,' she said, and Len, whose legs were a bit tired, held on to the hand-rail and pulled himself over it, and went up rather slowly until, there on the next landing he met her again, scrubbing away at a step. This landing was wide and to reach the next flight he had to pass an open lift-door.

'Oh no, oh no,' said Len to himself, 'it's climbing for me,' and though his calves were killing him and his ankles were now numb, he managed to heave himself over the old woman's step.

'She must get ahead of me by travelling on the lift,' he thought.

And this went on until he got to the seventy-fifth floor where again there was an open lift. This time the old woman could be heard scrubbing a step high up on the next flight.

'I've had enough of this,' Len said. 'My knees are weak as paper and that old girl is enough to tempt anyone to be rude. If it's a civil tongue I've got to have, there's only one thing for it – I'll take the lift the rest of the way. After all, who's to tell on me?'

And saying this, he crept into the open door of the nearest lift, pressed the button that said, 'Roof only' and . . . *dropped*. Down, down in the lift, faster than light, faster than sound, down to the cellars below the basement, and rolled out, as the lift-doors opened – in the shape of a small, black pebble!

And there he stayed.

Now you might imagine that his brother Les would have been worried when he didn't return. But he wasn't. He was very pleased, he saw it paving the way for himself. It was Arnie who went to the police, and, as they could find nothing out, it was he who took over Len's fish-stall and ran it along with his own until such time as his sharp brother could be found.

It wasn't long before Les was trying his luck with the Magician. With his head full of the golden pig and his ears dinning with the richness of red-gold and rubies he crossed the square and entered the saloon bar, where the landlord was busily drawing foaming pints for his regular customers.

These regulars were a devilish looking crowd, and when they saw Les they began to snicker among themselves, but he did not notice them – especially as the landlord was very civil to him when Les said that he'd come to ask for his daughter's hand.

The Magician said the same thing to him that he had to his brother.

And Les, wild with excitement stuttered and said, 'Oh yes, your pig-ship, I mean lordship, my highly honoured publican, sir. I do understand. No, your ruby-ship, I won't even look at a lift – feet all the time. Civil tongue, sir. Of course, sir. No cheating! What a hurtful suggestion,' and gave an artful, ingratiating smile, and left the bar, bowing to right and left as if acknowledging his dearest friends, while the strange regulars shook with mirth.

'He would marry my golden pig, would he? We'll see about that,' said the Magician as the door closed behind him.

And soon enough, Les arrived in his van at the block of skyscraper flats, and soon like Len before him, he was mounting the stairs. Up he went. Not as fast as Len had done. Steadily, using his artful wits to conserve his strength, but even so, by the time he had mounted some twenty flights he was certainly tired. That was when he met the old woman scrubbing as before. 'Look out,' she called, 'mind my step. Don't tread on my step, I've just cleaned it.'

He wasn't very pleased, but he remembered about a civil tongue, so he just said he was sorry and stepped carefully over the wet step.

She was on the next flight, then the next and

the one after that. She was still there when he reached the eighty-second flight. By now he was huffing and puffing as much as his brother Len had been; now his calves were weak as paper and his ankles bent inwards from the strain.

And there was the horrible old woman, scrubbing and complaining. 'Mind out, mind out,' she yelled. 'Don't tread on my step. What do you want to come up this way for? What do you think the lifts are for?'

At last Les showed his temper – he'd lost it long ago. 'Trying to tempt me to use the lift, eh?' he snarled. 'To blazes with your horrible bucket.'

And in spite of his tiredness, he raised his foot, and aimed a strong kick that sent the old woman's bucket bumping away down the steps, rolling across the landings, and clattering down the next flight, and the next and the next ... and after the bucket, down, down and down bounced a round black stone, falling from step to step along landings and down again till it descended to the cellars below the basement where it rolled and came to a stop beside a black stone that was already lying there.

Yes, Les was now a black pebble like his brother Len, and there they lay, side by side, on the floor of the lowest cellar of the tall block of flats.

So poor Arnie was left all alone to mind the three market-stalls as best he could. Across the square the golden pig still glowed with rubies, the Magician's waistcoat still flashed and sparkled, and his lovely daughter still brushed her moonlight hair.

The police from five counties began chasing clues – they had a theory that Len and Les had been members of a smuggling gang. They had carefully searched the abandoned vans and found nothing but cods' heads and fish-scales in the one and old potatoes and withered leeks in the other; but they were far from satisfied.

Now Arnie was very busy indeed. He felt he must keep his brothers' businesses going as well as his own so, as his only day off was Sunday, he had to leave it until then before he in his turn tried his hand at wooing the Magician's daughter.

But unlike Len and Les, Arnie did not go to the Magician. After all, it wasn't him he wanted to marry. No, he waited about the empty market square for an hour or so while he plucked up courage, and then he crossed the road, walked past the pub's swinging doors, and went in round the back through the gates the brewers' lorries used.

Here in the yard, he found the landlord's daughter, busily stacking dirty glasses in a vast washing-up machine. He was surprised to see how short she was – even with her heaped mass of hair – and glad to see how sweet she was – even sweeter than he'd imagined her to be when he'd fallen in love.

Awkwardly, because he was so overcome with emotion, he poured out his proposal:

'If you will marry me,' he said, 'I'll take you away from all this. We will live in the little cottage in the woods that my godmother left me – I'll cut wood and make chairs and tables, beds and cupboards for it. And a strong oak cradle to rock our babies in.

'And you,' he said sentimentally, 'will sit all day on the doorstep brushing your moonbeam hair.'

'I,' said the landlord's daughter practically, 'will be on the telephone or dictating letters to my secretary. I will be selling all the lovely furniture that you will go on making after we are married.'

She smiled at him, and he saw that her eyes were like sapphires, and her lips were like rubies. 'I fell in love with you a long time ago,' she said. 'I used to watch you when I was brushing my hair. How you stared! That's why I took so long doing it in the morning – I brushed it for you.

'I know you are a dreamy impractical fellow,' she said lovingly, 'or you'd never have let your brothers get in first. But that suits me very well, for I have a managing, business head on me.'

So they embraced, there in the yard before the washing-up machine full of glasses and tankards, and it was there the Magician found them.

The Magician stood regarding them for a moment and then he gave a loud cough, so that they sprang apart and looked sheepish. His daughter, however, quickly recovered her wits:

'You might as well know it, Dad,' she said, 'Arnie and I are engaged to be married.'

The Magician gave a sour smile. 'He hasn't asked me for my permission,' he said. 'Why didn't you?' he said to Arnie, 'why didn't you speak to me first?'

Arnie turned cherry-red, but he held his ground, polite to his future father-in-law he intended to be, but he wasn't going to be brow-beaten. 'I wasn't really interested in what you thought, sir,' he said. 'It's what your daughter thought that mattered. After all, if she hadn't cared for me you couldn't have made her marry me against her will. Not in this day and age, anyway.'

The Magician's daughter laughed, and squeezed his arm. 'Well said,' she told him.

'No, Dad,' she said to her father. 'You know you couldn't have forced me. Just what would you have done if one of Arnie's brothers had been successful? I wouldn't have considered either of them for a minute. You'd have had to part with your waistcoat or your pub-sign in lieu of me, I'm thinking.'

'It was hardly likely either of them would have succeeded anyway,' the Magician said, ' – neither of them had the character for success. I doubt very much if this one could manage to get the silver egg either – no one has ever beaten me at my own game, and I've a trick or two up my sleeve believe me.'

'The lengths you'll go to keep that nasty old sign and that flashy old waistcoat,' said his daughter scornfully.

'But I don't want either of them,' said Arnie mildly. 'All I ever wanted was your beautiful daughter. And it looks as if I've got her, anyway.'

The Magician thought for a moment, and then he smiled, and then he laughed. Out from the saloon bar swarmed the Magician's regulars – and they were laughing too.

Suddenly the Sunday bells began to chime from the church steeple, sending a whole flock of white pigeons up into the air from the belfry tower.

Suddenly the whole square was filled with little girls in white pinafores trotting off to Sunday School, and sweet old ladies and gentlemen in their Sunday best hobbling to church.

'So it's no silver egg, eh?' asked the Magician.

For answer his daughter put two fingers to her ruby lips and whistled shrill as any street-boy.

At once the air was filled with the beating

sound of great wings, the daylight darkened as something passed between the earth and the sun. There was a clicking of claws and a scraping of quills, and suddenly the yard was filled with the stuffy dusty feathers of a vast and stupid-looking bird – a bird that was trying to balance itself upon the washing-up machine.

'The wishing-bird,' said the Magician's daughter proudly. 'No need to climb if you know the correct signal.

'Lay an egg for us,' she said commandingly, and the stupid creature did just that – laid a fine silver egg that rolled into the washing-up machine and lay among the wet glasses.

'And something else?' said the Magician's daughter. The bird opened its beak, and there on its tongue lay two black pebbles.

'Your brothers I think,' she said to Arnie.

Then, to her father, 'Come on now, Dad, change them back and don't mess about.'

Looking thoroughly abashed in front of his regulars, whose admiring glances were fixed on his resolute child, the Magician obliged by making a few magic passes and muttering a few strange words.

And there, dishevelled from their adventure, and damp from having travelled in the bird's mouth, stood Len and Les! Both it is to be hoped, wiser and better men.

Next day they returned to their stalls in the market, and in spite of the suspicions of the police they conducted themselves so well that in time they became prosperous from their own industry. Whilst Len never could afford a jewelled waistcoat, he managed to buy himself a real dazzler of a watch and chain with charms and dangleums of gold encrusted with jewels. Les eventually moved into a very big greengrocer's shop, with a sign overhead of a golden pineapple. It was only gold-leaf to be sure, but he made up for it by having a fat little wife upon whom he bestowed a real ruby necklace and a ruby ring.

And Arnie and the Magician's daughter? They went to live in the little house in the woods as Arnie had hoped. Arnie makes furniture from the trees in the wood, and the Magician's daughter manages the sales. They are both very happy, and every night Arnie sits entranced as he watches her brush her moonlight hair.

The Magician Who Kept a Pub

Len and Les and the Magician are now great friends – they spend many hours in the saloon bar talking over old times, or standing treat to the regulars.

As for the stupid wishing-bird she still sits on top of the high tower-block laying her silver eggs. You might try getting one for yourself some time – that is, if you can manage such a climb and can keep your patience with that old woman.

2

The Giant Who Wanted to Eat Boys

A TIME came when there was only one giant left in the world.

This giant lived in a castle on top of a high hill; a green moss-covered castle full of empty rooms where only the giant spiders moved as they spun their everlasting webs and cut out the sunlight.

Some days the giant sat still and did nothing from morning to night, but there were days when he walked about his castle. When he did this:

> the earth shook, the trees clashed
> the rocks danced, the streams dashed,

and the people who lived in the valley below looked up and said, 'The Old Giant is walking about upstairs!' and they laughed and went on with what they were doing.

The village baker didn't laugh though. He was a thoughtful man. He'd pause in his work, and look at his dough, and shake his head and say, 'So long as he doesn't walk this way!' But nobody took any notice of him.

Sometimes the giant sang to himself. He could only remember one song – a nursery-rhyme for baby giants, so he always sang that:

> 'Hot Cross Boys, Hot Cross Boys.
> One-a-penny, two-a-penny,
> HOT CROSS BOYS.'

He sang very loudly and stamped his great feet to the time, till the earth shook,

> the trees clashed and clashed
> the rocks danced and danced
> the streams dashed and dashed,

and the people who lived in the valley below looked up and said, 'That's the Old Giant making a noise upstairs!' and they laughed and went on with what they were doing.

The people who lived in the valley knew about the giant, but as the giant knew nothing about them they felt very safe.

'He might find out one day and then what?'
the baker would say to himself as he banged and
battered the dough.

Now, the only food the giant had to eat was
bread-and-cheese or cheese-and-bread. Nothing
more. He got very tired of that.

So, before he sat down to a meal he'd cheer
himself up with his song:

'Hot Cross Boys, Hot Cross Boys.
Be they fatter, be they thinner,
They will make a tasty dinner:
HOT CROSS BOYS!'

As he picked up his piece of coarse brown
bread and bit into his lump of hard yellow
cheese, he'd sigh and say: 'Oh, I wonder what
boys *are*? I wonder what they taste like? THEY
DO SOUND NICE.'

Then, one day when the giant was walking
about his castle and annoying the giant spiders
by breaking their webs as he did so, he tripped
over something that was lying on the floor
among the cobwebs. 'Ho-ho,' he said. 'What's
this?'

He bent down and picked it up. It was a dirty
metal tube with a filthy piece of glass at each
end of it.

'Why, it's a spy-glass!' cried the giant. 'I'd
forgotten there were such things! I can have fun
with this!'

He cleaned the pipe on his sleeve and polished
the glass at each end with his tie.

'What do I do now?' he thought. 'It's so long
ago since I held a spy-glass in my hands.'

At last he put it to his eye and looked through the big end straight at one of the giant spiders, and the giant spider seemed very small up there on its web: no more than a speck, he could hardly see it.

'Oh-ho,' said the giant, 'that's a funny thing!' He turned the spy-glass round and looked through the small end and there was the giant spider waving his legs in anger, and the giant spider looked enormous – big as a giant elephant, frightening as a giant octopus!

'Ugh,' said the giant, 'I don't think much of you! I'll take a look out of the window and see if there is anything better to see outside.'

And he beat and brushed away the cobwebs that covered the window, opened it, and leaned out with his spy-glass to his eye and looked down on to the valley below, at the green fields and red-roofed houses of the village.

He twiddled and twisted the spy-glass till the houses looked bigger and BIGGER. Then he saw PEOPLE. People working, walking, running, talking and going about their daily affairs never dreaming that they were being watched.

The giant fiddled with the spy-glass turning

it more and more until the people looked
HUGE.

'Giants!' bellowed the giant. 'So I'm not the
only one! And they were there all the time! How
happy they look and how well fed they appear
to be. I don't suppose they have to live on bread-
and-cheese as I do. I expect they have Hot Cross
Boys whenever they fancy them.'

He thought very hard: 'I'm sure they do!'

He thought harder still. 'I know what I'll do,
I'll go and ask if they could spare me some.'

He laughed out loud, and dropping the spy-
glass he went out of the castle and down to the
valley below, singing as he went:

> 'Hot Cross Boys, Hot Cross Boys!
> Bite them, crunch them,
> Chew and munch them –
> HOT CROSS BOYS!'

And as he went down the earth cracked, the
trees fell, the rocks rolled and the streams over-
flowed and everything tumbled and gushed to
the valley.

'The giant is coming! The giant is coming!'
the people cried, and they dropped everything

they were doing and ran away to find somewhere
to hide.

'What shall we do? What shall we do?' they
wailed as they clambered into lofts or buried
themselves in straw-heaps.

'We'll have to wait and see what he's after,'
said the baker, putting aside his dough and going off to hide in a flour-bin. But he left it open
at the top so that he could peep at the giant.

When the giant arrived at the village there
was no one in sight, and all he could see were
the little houses around his feet.

'Where have the giants gone?' he said sadly.
'Who is there to offer me a dish of Hot Cross
Boys?'

And he began to cry. Enormous sobs shook
him, and great tears ran down his face and fell in
puddles or splashed on the roofs below.

The people, hearing the giant crying and the
sound of tears pattering on their roofs, crept out
of hiding and peeped round corners at him.

The tear-puddles grew larger and larger. Soon
they joined and became one puddle and then
they began to flow down the street. 'He will
flood our houses,' they whispered to one

another. 'What is wrong with him? We must do something to stop him weeping like this.'

But nobody offered to confront the giant.

Until at last the baker, who all this time had been peeping from his flour-bin and thinking hard, crept out from hiding, and began to dust some of the flour from his clothes, saying: 'I'll speak to him. But it's no use saying anything from down here. I will go into the church – it's our highest building, and if someone will give me a leg-up, I'll climb to the top of the steeple. If I shout he should hear me from there.'

And that's just what happened.

Suddenly, in the middle of his weeping, the giant heard a little shout: 'Do you want any help, sir?' it said.

The giant looked downwards and saw a tiny floury man clinging to the church steeple. The steeple came just up to his knee, so he bent his head to see and hear better. 'I hoped I would find some giants,' he said sadly. 'I – I hoped they would ask me to dinner!

'All I have in my green-mossy castle is bread-and-cheese and I'm so tired of that.'

He spoke in such a mournful voice that the

people came right out from their hiding places and stood in the open to stare. The giant looked at them in amazement, then, seeing they seemed afraid of him, he said kindly, 'I only wanted some boys to eat. I've never tasted boys.' And to show them what he meant he began to sing:

> 'Hot Cross Boys, Hot Cross Boys!
> One-a-penny, two-a-penny,
> HOT CROSS BOYS.'

He'd hardly opened his mouth to sing, when all the boys of the village took to their heels and sped away in all directions, and all the villagers shrieked.

The giant stopped singing. 'Why did they do that?' he asked.

'They are BOYS. They don't want you to eat them,' said the baker sternly.

'Oh dear,' said the giant. 'I didn't know boys were like that. They will be hard to catch, and very wriggly to eat. Still, I understand they make a *very tasty dinner*!'

When he said that, the people fell on their knees and pleaded: 'Please don't eat our boys.'

'Surely you can spare me one or two,' said the giant. 'Surely you don't want to keep all those hot cross boys for yourselves?'

The people were silent with horror. Only the baker spoke – or rather, shouted. 'You can have all the Hot Cross Boys you like, sir,' he yelled politely, and the people groaned.

'He doesn't want our boys,' cried the quick-witted baker. 'He wants HOT CROSS BOYS, and I'm the man to make them.

'Just sit down in that field over there, sir,' he called to the giant, 'and I will make you some right away.'

So the giant went to the field and sat down on a haystack while the baker slid down from the church steeple and hurried off to his bake-house.

He mixed some dough. He rolled it flat. Then, he took up his knife and he cut out lots and lots of bun-boys: big ones and small ones – fat ones and thin ones! He stuck in currant eyes and cherry noses and bits of peel-turned-down-at-the-corners for mouths. Then he put them into the oven to bake.

When they were ready he took them out to the

giant. They were very, very hot and with all their mouths turned down they looked very, very cross.

'There!' said the clever baker, 'HOT CROSS BOYS!'

'They *do* look good,' said the happy giant, and he settled himself on the haystack and ate and ate and ate.

The baker made more and more and more Hot Cross Boys and all the people ran backwards and forwards carrying the trays of Hot Cross Bun-Boys to the hungry giant.

It was almost nightfall when at last the giant said, 'I'm full up!'

He got up very slowly, because he was so full, and he said, 'Isn't it funny? Now I've eaten so many Hot Cross Boys, I don't think I'll want to taste any more as long as I live. There's a lot to be said for cheese-and-bread!'

And back he went to his castle, slowly and carefully because he was so full, so slowly and carefully that not a tree trembled, not a rock quivered, not a stream rippled, while in the valley the people cheered from relief.

And after that the giant never sang again,

although he often looked out of his castle window and watched the people through his spy-glass.

As for the clever baker he made many bun-boys after that. But he put the peel for their mouths with the corners turning up.

He called them HOT SMILING BOYS and they were so good they sold like hot cakes!

3

Romany Revenge

'YOU wouldn't like to cross a gypsy, eh?' asked old Joe. 'Ah, they're a real revengeful lot all right. Long memories they have. Still – ' he laughed and spat into a rosebed.

'There's a crowd that used to come to our place when I were a lad. Mumpusses they was. Old Granny Mumpus and her lot. Every year, sharp on Michaelmas they'd turn up regular as a clock to give a hand with the plucking of the geese. For folk went in strong for Michaelmas geese in them days, and my old Mother had orders from miles around. In fact it was my Mother's poultry and dairy-stuff that kept us going, for our Dad was too taken up with his roses to give much time to farming.

'Old Granny Mumpus was a real Romany – nigh on a hundred by all accounts by the time I got to know her, with quick skinny fingers and her old pipe burning like a bonfire, and half a dozen great-grandsons and their wives taking orders from her meek as meek.

'I can see her now, squatting in our barn beside a great heap of feathers, and, "Lady," she'd say to our Mother, "you'll spare a few feathers to make a gypsy's bed lie easy?"

' "Of course," our Mother would say. "I'll sort you out a bag full, and young Joe here shall bring them over along with the pie and the you-know-what."

'You see, our Mother always made a special big veal-and-ham pie for the Mumpusses because she knew the old lady was partial to pies of that nature, and knowing how nosy I was about gypsy-doings my Mother always arranged it so's I should have an excuse for going over among the caravans.

'Carrying the pie in both hands, with the you-know-what (which in case you *don't* know was our Mother's way of naming all the Mumpusses' earnings, tied up in a bit of brown paper), tucked inside my shirt, I picked my way across the camp ground, with all the Mumpusses looking at me, the boys a-glaring and the gals a-poking out their fingers, their dogs a-snapping, and their old pot a-bubbling over a fire, and their rough old horses on tethers fit to trip you. Like a royal butler – carrying the pie to the old queen gypsy's van, pretending not to see anything, but taking everything in!

'You never saw such a bed as old Granny Mumpus had! Two great red-and-white twill bags one atop the other, and stuffed to busting. The old lady would rip out a few stitches along

the side of one or other of the bags and claw in the new lot of feathers, and somehow there was always just room for them!

'They always camped down in our bottom meadow, and might have gone on doing so, only the old lady was taken ill with pneumony and died sudden in the County Hospital.

'Tobe – he was her eldest grandson – took over then. (Tobe's Pa had married a girl from down Asingforth – one of the them Hacketts – bad blood in that lot – so Tobe as you might say was no true Romany.) That was when you realized how strong a hand the old lady had had, for, from being a reliable and more-or-less trustworthy lot, such as could be relied on for seasonal jobs all over the four counties, they became real terrors, poaching, thieving, threatening and always in and out of jail.

'The first year old Dad asked them along for their old Granny's sake, but seeing there was some half-dozen hens and a piglet unaccounted for afterwards, he wouldn't let them nigh the place again. Three years running they turned up hopeful at geese-plucking time, but old Dad wouldn't be moved, and finally they gave up.

Not before that Tobe had cussed and sworn to have his own back, though.'

Old Joe laughed again.

'Gypsies' revenge like! Well, a couple of years after we'd thought to have seen the last of the Mumpusses, old Dad entered our garden for the County Rose Show. It was the first year he'd done so, along of his not wishing to try his hand until he was sure of beating the other competitors. Old Dad was like that. All or nothing for him. And, having seen how the judging had gone in previous years, and knowing just what he was likely to be up against, he felt there was just about every chance of his winning the County Cup. Everyone thought so too, for, in spite of old Mother's nag-nagging about the waste of time it was, it seemed that in rose-growing circles my Father was well looked up to.

'You can imagine what a time we had getting ready for the show, us children weeding the paths and taking stones off the beds – even our old Mum got carried away by the excitement, and got down on her knees and scrubbed the stonework round the little pond.

'I must say it looked a treat though. By the second week in June when the judging took place it was at its best. Ramblers, tree-climbers, standards, and little dwarf fellows as small as shirt-buttons my old Dad grew – and they were blazing away in every colour a rose could be coaxed to grow in. As for the scent – it reached for miles around.

'I had a fight with a boy at school who reckoned I smelled of them. I saw to it his smeller didn't work for a day or two, I can tell you,' old Joe grinned. 'They were times all right.

'The night before the show we turned in early, for we were worn out. I remember sleeping very deep, and only stirring the once when I heard the sound of horses going down the bottom lane, and then going to sleep quick before I could give the sound a name, like.

'We got up extra early too, and it was natural for my Father to go off at once to see his garden, even though it was hardly light enough to see by. "Go along with him, Joe boy," said our Mother, "or he'll forget to be back for the milking."

'So we strolled through the yard and down to the garden. We couldn't believe our eyes! "It's been snowing," I said at last, which was plain daft because the weather was hot as hot for the time of year.

'Still, it looked as near to a snowfall as I was ever to see! Old Dad went staggering forward and picked up some of the stuff and "Feathers!" he yelled, "Feathers!"

'Yes, there were millions and millions of feathers that had been tossed and scattered all over the rose garden: on every bush and shrub and climber, down all the paths and clinging to every spider's web. All the paths were covered and the little ornamental pond was choked up. You couldn't see the roses for fluff!

'When poor old Dad got back to the house he was shaking all over. It took him some time to gasp out the story because of the shock. "Feathers," he said to our Mother. "The garden – ruined! It'll take months to get rid of them!"

'Old Mother went back with us to see for herself. It was lighter by then. She took a quick look.

' "Gypsies. Those Mumpusses!" she said, "Look here!" she pointed out a little old red-and-white rag that was caught up on a briar. "I'd know that twill anywhere! Old Granny Mumpus' feather-bed!"

' "The horses, I thought I heard horses last night," I said.

' "That Tobe said they'd be having their revenge on me!" said our Dad. "But they'll pay for this. Spoiling my garden and my chance for the cup. They must have heard I stood to win it."

'Then: "*They'll pay for it all right,*" said our Mother suddenly, "for look at this here, Dad."

'She sounded so excited that even Dad hurried forward to see what she was pointing to. "Look, Dad," says our Mother, "do you see what I see? Money – look!"

'Then we saw that mixed up with all those feathers were lots of bits of paper, five-pound, pound and the old-fashioned ten-shilling notes and here and there a sprinkle of golden sovereigns.

' "That must have been the old lady's savings," said our Mother. She looked at us all,

standing there, staring our eyes out. "Come on, help me gather it up," says she, "the milking can wait for once."

'Yes,' said old Joe, 'the gypsies had their revenge on us all right, but as old Mum said, they paid for it. They never knew it, but it cost them six thousand, three hundred and twenty-eight pounds. All the tribe's earnings that the old lady had hidden away.'

4

The Witch Who Lived on the Motorway

THIS story is about a wicked witch who lived on a motorway.

They don't usually let people live on motorways, but this witch's cottage had been there centuries before the motorway was laid and she had refused to move from it. Several important people had tried to make her change her mind, but she had done so many nasty things to them with her magic that they decided in the end to leave her alone.

So there she stayed, full of spiteful tricks and harmful ideas for dealing with anyone who bothered her. Her tumbledown cottage with its grimy brickwork was a disgrace to the tidy carriageways and graceful new bridges, and her weed-choked garden a blot on the neat verges.

By day the sight of her dirty face glaring from a window filled the passing drivers with dread, and at night time, when she brewed her spells, the steam from her iron pot ran like mist along the road surface as far as the nearest service station where it spoiled the taste of the tea and sandwiches in the Transport Cafeteria and made the lorry drivers grumble.

At first the authorities erected signs along the track saying things like BEWARE WITCH 20M AHEAD NO STOPPING – with a black cut-out of a hook-nosed witch on a broomstick underneath for the benefit of foreigners, and drivers who couldn't read. The one before you reached her was enormous:

WITCH ¼ MILE AHEAD
STOP AT YOUR PERIL!

Even so at first accidents happened and risks were taken. Vehicles broke down on the track-way near her dwelling. In consequence many a luxuriant head of hair had scorched and shrivelled from the blast of her glance; and many a distraught driver had returned bald to his grieving family. Lorry drivers forced to pull in to cool over-heated engines drove off again minus their ears or with over-sized noses obscuring their vision, or faces turned green as grass. It was a grave situation.

The scandal came to a head one dreadful day when the witch turned an outing of Women's Institute ladies into a coachload of hens, and their driver arrived back at the village with a bus full of eggs and feathers, with every lady perched on the back of her seat clucking with pride.

From then on the roadside witch-warning signs said HAVE YOU CHECKED YOUR VEHICLE? as well, and the AA and RAC set up special check-points for faint-hearted motorists. Of course the transport drivers ignored these signs, but none the less it was noticed that that stretch of the motorway became known for exemplary lorry-driving, and that not one lorry failed its MOT test!

Soon, so good was the organization, so careful the authorities, that the witch's verges were kept clear and she was no longer regarded as a hazard. Only the nasty-tasting food and drink in the cafeteria remained as a reminder of her malevolence and anyway the drivers blamed that on a succession of canteen manageresses who came and went with monotonous regularity.

So the witch was left alone – except, of course, by children. No child who knows there's a witch about can resist going for a peep. Many children visited the service station with their parents, and now and again, while the adults were sitting over their lunches or doing exercises to loosen up after their long drives, a child or so would stroll across the fields for a quick look. Children who did this were never seen again. The moment they approached her cottage the wicked witch seized her magic broom and rushed out and swept them up and shovelled them into her coal-cellar. She kept them there and fed them on crumbs and crusts and scrapings from the pots, and vowed they would never see daylight again.

One day she captured a girl who hadn't come to spy on her at all. This was a girl called Emily Brown, whose Dad was a lorry driver. He had been bringing her back from a holiday with her Grannie. Emily had wandered off to look for rose-hips for her Mum to make into syrup for the baby, while her Dad played bar-billiards in the Transport Cafeteria. She had half-filled a plastic bag by the time she reached the field behind the witch's cottage.

The rose-hips shone like cherries in the hedge that bounded the witch's garden, and Emily, reaching up to pick them, glimpsed the streaked window-glass and tattered curtains of the house; but she was completely unaware of the malevolent eyes fixed on her through the shreds of net.

'Someone doesn't like housework,' poor Emily thought, as she fixed her bag into a convenient crotch in the hedge. 'Can't cook, either,' as the thick, unpleasant smell of the bubbling brew crept through the close, thorny branches. 'Ah well, no one there likely to want these hips!' she thought happily.

So engrossed she was, pressing down the scarlet berries to accommodate another handful, so glad to think of her Mum's pleasure, that she did not hear the slip-slop of ill-shod feet running across the meadow grass . . .

The rustle of hedgerow trees absorbed the hiss of the furious breath of the oncoming witch. It was only when a black shadow fell across her bag of pickings and the hot breath scorched her back that Emily became aware of her peril – but by then it was too late to flee!

In a moment she was pounced upon. 'Spying, are you?' the witch shrieked. Emily's scream of fear was stifled in her throat by the swiftness of her passage across the littered yard.

There was the rasp of a key in a rusty lock, a groan of hinges, a thrust into smelly darkness, and Emily had joined the other captives who came from the coaly depths to mingle their tears with hers, while the witch, screaming for joy, danced about her backyard. 'I've got Emily Brown!' she cried. 'Emily Brown is MINE.'

Mr Brown paled as those terrible shouts reached his ears, but there was nothing he could do to save his daughter. He would just have to return home and break the news to the rest of his family.

The Browns were very upset about Emily. The younger children cried and would not be comforted. As for Mrs Brown, she flew at her husband and said he didn't deserve to have such a loving and thoughtful child as poor Emily had been – gathering hips for her Mum while he was messing about playing games with his mates!

Mr Brown said if Mrs Brown had been contented with the syrup you buy at the chemists, instead of always mucking about making up her Mother's old recipes, Emily would never have thought of going off, and they rowed and wrangled, and the babies wept, until at last Davie, the eldest boy, who was training to be a plumber's mate, decided to rescue his sister for the sake of peace and quiet.

Now, all trades have their secrets, and

plumbers are no exception. Plumbers pass their secrets on from boss to apprentice. Being a plumber's trainee-mate, Davie had learned a few things about witches that only plumbers know. Now, for the sake of peace in the home, and because he missed his sister, he started to plan how he could use his trade secrets in order to get Emily out of the witch's clutches.

First, he went to see his Granddad, to ask for a loan of his binoculars and his second-best watch. Then, knowing that his Dad's next route would require him to halt at the service station near the witch's house, he took those binoculars and his bag of tools and climbed into the back of the lorry and hid under a tarpaulin. He did not want his parents to know what he was up to, in case they tried to stop him.

As soon as his Dad had parked the lorry outside the Transport Cafeteria and had gone in to get a cup of the nasty-tasting tea and one of the doubtful sandwiches that was all they could offer, Davie slipped off from the back and made his way across the fields to a spot where he could see the witch's house in the far distance.

Then he carefully trained his glasses on to the

cottage. From window to window his gaze went and at last he gave a satisfied grunt. A large window with a frosted-glass pane! That must be the witch's bathroom!

Now one of the secrets Davie had learned was that by the nature of their evil works witches get very dirty. It takes them a long time to clean themselves again. They need lots of soap and water and scrubbing-brushes, but clean they must be or their magic dries up! So, every witch however situated has a good large bathroom.

Another thing Davie had been taught was that by the time it's six o'clock in the evening witches have become so dirty that this is the time their magic powers are at their weakest. So this is the time they take their baths.

He also knew that a bag of plumber's tools are a good shield against weak magic.

So Davie propped his Granddad's watch upon a grass tussock in front of him and waited until it was six pm, then, taking up his tool-bag he made his way boldly to the witch's front-gate, pushed it open and strolled into the tangled garden and began to look about him.

The wicked witch was just going to have her bath when she spied Davie wandering round her place.

'I'll be after you when I've had my scrub-up,' she screeched. 'I'll sweep you up with my magic broom and shovel you into my cellar, Davie Brown!

'I'll keep you there, and feed you on crusts and crumbs and scrapings from the pots just like the other children. Don't think you can escape me with your plumber's bag and your cheek. WHEN I'M CLEAN I HAVE THE POWER OF THE DEVIL!' And she began to claw and tear at her witch's garments she was in such a hurry to get undressed.

But Davie Brown was as cool as a cucumber. 'I know how to stop your magic capers,' he said under his breath, and, with all the ease in the world he strolled round the house looking for the lid of the water stop-cock in the backyard.

Meanwhile the wicked old witch had kicked aside the last of her smelly rags and had turned on the taps: the hot one and the cold one.

'Brown soap on scrubbing brushes is the best thing for washing witches,' she crooned. 'Oh

Davie Brown, striding like a bantam-cock around my house with your miserable little plumber's bag! Little do you know that once I am clean my magic will be as strong and wicked as ever!'

But Davie Brown was busy in the backyard poking among a tangle of stinging-nettles. Even as the old witch cackled, he found what he was looking for. Under a dock plant lay the water cock's iron lid. Taking a hook from his plumber's bag, he crooked it through the lid and lifted it off. Then he spread out his plumber's apron and knelt down on it, and, putting his hand down the hole HE TURNED OFF THE WATER SUPPLY with the special plumber's key. Then he put the iron lid on again. After that he went round the yard and collected all the old junk and rubbish he could find – heavy things like old millstones and broken wringers and piled them on top.

'If she doesn't have a bath soon her magic will dry up and she won't be able to make any more spells,' Davie Brown said. 'It won't matter how many washes she has after that, the magic will have evaporated!'

And, just as the old witch climbed into the bath, the taps stopped running. There was a dying hiss of steam, a feeble icy drop and then no more water!

'Where's the water gone?' moaned the wicked old witch. 'It was here a moment ago. Hot and cold mixed – just right for washing.' She turned the taps on fuller, but no water came.

'I must have a bath! I must!' she screeched. 'I must get rid of my grime!'

Davie Brown heard her yelling, and so did the children locked in the coal-cellar. They began to beat on the bars of the cellar-grating.

'I've done it! I've done it!' Davie cried, and the hidden children raised a feeble cheer.

Davie went into the cottage, found the cellar and opened the door. 'Come on, our Em!' he said. 'If we nip across the fields quickly we'll have time to meet our Dad's lorry when it stops on the homeward trip.'

He picked up his plumber's bag and his Granddad's watch and binoculars and they scurried off across the fields, followed by the other children, all dirty from having sat on the coal for so long, but no one as dirty as the miserable

old witch! Shouting with joy they streamed across the fields behind Davie Brown.

What a sight of rejoicing there was as the children tumbled into the Transport Cafeteria. How the lorry drivers cheered! At once a team of volunteers undertook to take the children to their several homes.

Mr Brown, overjoyed at the sight of Emily and the prospect of a peaceful home-life again, beamed with joy.

'I don't know how you did it, lad,' he said warmly, shaking Davie by the hand.

'It's just a trade secret, Dad,' Davie told him modestly. 'Anyway, I can assure you her magic days are over – she won't make any more nasty spells or put children in among her coals.'

And she didn't. After the children had gone the old witch climbed out of her bath and put on a tattered dressing-gown and went to the yard and began to move the rubbish from the iron lid. Then she raised it, and turned the water on again.

As the bath filled up she washed herself and washed herself, soaped and scrubbed and rubbed herself for hours until she was shining and clean.

But it made no difference. Her magic had dried up!

'Oh well,' said the old witch, 'I'll just have to find another way of making a living!'

So she cleaned her house and whitewashed the walls. She weeded the garden and tidied the yard. She made a neat little roadway running off the motorway and leading to the back of the cottage. Then she put a big sign at the entrance to the little roadway. This sign is there to this day; it shows a friendly-looking witch, holding a big tea-pot in one hand, and a steaming pie in the other. At this witch's feet a large arrow points in the direction of the cottage; above her head is written WITCHIE'S PULL-UP TRANSPORT DRIVERS ONLY FOOD LIKE MOTHER MAKES.

The cottage now looks so attractive and the witch's cooking is so good that all the vans and lorries turn off at her special roadway and the Transport Cafeteria at the service station has fallen to rack and ruin.

Mr Brown goes there regularly because he says Witchie makes the best steak and kidney pies and fries the crispest chips in the country –

and he should know: he's a long-distance driver.

Sometimes Davie Brown and his boss, the plumber, stop their van there and go inside for a cuppa.

The witch is always delighted to see them and insists that they try her newly-baked cakes and won't dream of taking a penny from them. It is obvious that she enjoys her altered station in life.

She says, 'No hard feelings, Davie.'

And Davie says, 'No hard feelings.'

And that's how it should be!

5

The Brighton Merman

Don't let anyone tell you that there are no such beings as mer-people. There are lots of them about, though nowadays the mermaids tend to keep far off-shore and only swim in at high tide on very dark nights.

It's the mermen who are the bold ones. They are about in the day-time as well. They drift in with the tide, just below the surface of the water. Camouflaged by great tangles of sea-weed they mix with the bathers and listen to their conversation, or bobbing their great heads up and down among the mooring buoys, spy on the holiday-makers on the seaside beaches.

You may say that *you* have never seen a merman when you've been at the seaside but I doubt if you've ever really looked for one; and in any case, remember that the mer-people are protected by centuries of cunning!

It may surprise you to know that the mermen

strongly disapprove of our beach behaviour.
They have very sensitive ears and they loathe
our badly tuned transistors, and they hate the
litter that drifts in and out on every tide – all
our nasty plastic ice-cream tubs, straws, beer-
cans and the like.

Mermen spread terrible stories about us all
over the seabed. They think we are a pretty
scandalous lot with our sunbathing and horse-
play and keep a strict eye on the timid mermaids when they venture in at night-time.
Occasionally though a more enlightened and
tolerant one does surface – one who pities
rather than despises us and is prepared to point
out that there appear to be two distinct species
of humans – those who sprawl on beaches and
appear to be idlers, and the busy inlanders who
are engaged in numberless activities.

There was once such a merman who regularly
came up along the Brighton coast. But then he
made a special study of our ways. From a
well-constructed hide of seaweed spotted with
gull-droppings he spent hours watching the
strange habits of humanity. Once many years
before, as a small merboy he had broken the

taboos of the underseas people and dived into
one of those great masses of weedy horror that
we call wrecks, where, probing among the
barnacled bones, he had discovered a pair of
fine binoculars in a waterproof case. These had
become his dearest treasure, and with their
assistance he was able to spend long hours
observing the strange ways of those other land-
people – the ones who didn't frolic in the sea,
sunbathe on the warm pebbles or shout: the
ordinary everyday people of Brighton going
about their day-to-day lives – the respectable
men in business suits, the prim ladies with dogs,
the well-behaved schoolchildren walking with
their teachers on the way to the museum, the
workmen building the new office blocks and
the people who served in the shops along the
front.

Day after day he rose and floated beneath
his hide, coming up by the high breakwater
beyond the West Pier, his sea-sharp eyes raking
the moving throng beyond the beach for
glimpses of the true Brighton folk. An occasional flash of binocular glass might have
betrayed his presence, but then – with all the

flash and dash of the spray about him – who would have suspected?

Soon like all watchers of an alien species, he began to recognize happenings and individuals and came to all sorts of wrong conclusions about them too. In fact, he became so crazy about the land and the land-people that when he was back among the sea-folk he could talk about nothing else. Nothing below sea satisfied him any more. He became a *landophile*!

Swimming through the underseas avenues he would gaze disparagingly upon the delicate shell-chariots drawn by plunging dolphins that have transported the Lords of the Sea from times immemorial and think longingly of the shiny smelly cars that he saw daily passing to and fro along the front.

'What speed the land-men can command!' he would say. 'Oh! To travel in an earth-dweller's chariot drawn by his mighty and invisible beasts!' (That, you will note, was one of the wrong conclusions.)

He swam in after dark too. In this way he was able to get into conversation with the evening strollers, who, seeing him half-submerged, took him for a late-night bather and stopped to chat with him and in this way he picked up a lot of misleading information, as he dared not ask direct questions in case he betrayed himself.

It was quite a point of pride with the merman that no one guessed who he really was. And he thought this was indeed a fact until one night, when he had just pulled himself up on to his usual breakwater, and was arranging his tail in a comfortable position below the water, a voice said, 'Say, man, you *are* a man mermaid, aren't you?'

He was so startled he nearly slipped from his perch. He looked in the direction the voice had come from but could see only what appeared to be a dark rock-mass.

As he stared the rock stirred and moved and got up and came towards him. Then he saw that it wasn't a rock at all, but a black boy dressed in a dark shirt and jeans.

'I'm sorry I made you jump like that,' the boy said. 'I thought you knew I was there!

'I often come down to the beach after dark when I've done my homework. I get tired of watching telly, so I slip out and come down here and watch in case the mermaids come in.

'I sit very still and very quiet. They never notice me because I am black and my clothes are dark. They are only interested in the coloured lights and the cars and the dancers on the pier, they point and whisper and giggle behind their fingers, but they never look my way.

'But you are different, you look all round you and you talk to people. I thought you'd picked me out long ago.'

The merman hadn't liked the shake-up he'd received when the boy had suddenly spoken, so, to cover his fright, he began to rage and bluster:

'How dare you spy upon our modest mer-maidens?' he thundered. 'There are few nights dark enough for them to venture near the shore for their innocent entertainment. Now you have ruined it for them. Now they can never come again!'

'But I haven't done anything,' the boy cried, 'I've only *looked*. The first time I saw them I was as startled as you were just now. I was just sitting there, watching the waves and thinking about my O-levels and wishing that the people in the flat under us weren't so mean about my practising the piano, when all of a sudden, in they came – rows of them like foam-bubbles in the darkness with their white faces all along the edges of the waves and their white arms around one another's shoulders. And whisper – whisper – whispering all the time.

'They are so pretty and playful I wouldn't disturb them for the world and when they splash about and frisk their tails and catch the colours from the promenade lights on their scales they look so happy I could watch them for ever. Now and again, one, who is a little bolder than the rest will sing a little bit of a song before the others hush her to whispers again. It's for the sake of those little snatches of song that I come down to the beach at night-time, for I've never heard anything so beautiful on land.

'That's how I came to pick you out,' the boy went on, 'I've seen you swim in and watched you speaking to people. At first I wasn't sure;

after all, plenty of fellows around the town have got great head-mops and beards like yours. But one night, when you thought no one was about I watched you picking the little fishes from between your scales and then I knew.'

The boy spoke so reasonably that the merman's anger died.

'Well,' he said, 'I suppose I can't blame you. We are always spying on you land-people. But our maids lead very sheltered lives and are easily frightened, so I'd be glad if you'd keep all this to yourself.'

'But of course I will,' the boy cried. 'I wouldn't want to do anything to spoil their pleasure. Oh please don't do anything to stop them coming! I'll never come down to the beach at night-time again, I promise, but please don't spoil it for them.'

By that time the moon was riding high above them, and the merman saw that the boy's face was as good and honest as his words. So he said, 'All right then – that will be our secret. And as for your watching – if you promise to keep it to yourself, I see no reason why you shouldn't come for a peep if you want to. Only it's no use coming on a night like this – moonlight or starlight either. Our girls only come in when it's pitchy-dark.'

Suddenly he began to laugh. 'They're so timid too! The flash of a night-flying gull can scatter them in a moment – so they'll streak for home at the turn of his white wing – and to think you've sat there night after night, dark as the darkness, watching without detection! Ho-ho-ho!'

The boy joined in the laughter.

'So you can stay at home and watch the thing you said on moonlit nights,' said the merman cheerfully.

'I don't know that I care about telly at all,' replied the boy. 'It's real lonesome in our flat in the evening with Mum and Dad out working and my young brothers fast asleep. If I could try out my music it wouldn't be so bad. There are tunes and songs running through my head all day, and not a chance to pick them over on the piano and try them out with the folk downstairs ready to bang their ceiling if I so much as creak open the keyboard.'

The merman was fascinated. This was talk of an alien life for which even his binocular-spying and evening chats with the strollers had not prepared him. It was as if a bird-watcher were to suddenly find himself conducting a conversation with a rare migrant whose habits he had been speculating upon for many seasons. Seizing upon an opportunity to ply the boy with questions about the town of Brighton and its people he said, 'Well, you can always come and talk to me. Talk to me now – tell me about this place where you live and about your family.'

So the boy told him about the flats on the other side of the railway, and the merman marvelled at the idea of people living above and below each other without sharing anything in common. 'This couldn't be in our ocean-world,' he exclaimed. 'We all live and eat and sleep together in our weed-padded caverns.'

'We have people like that too,' the boy told him. 'We call them drop-outs. My Mum says that's not the way for anyone to live. She says people have just got to be clean and decent and respectable, but, of course, she's only talking about the ones around *us*. I'm sure it's different for you.'

'Tell me about your parents,' said the merman. 'Tell me why they are not at home at night-time.'

'Mum and Dad work nights at the Royal Pavilion,' said the boy. 'The Royal Pavilion is the most famous and beautiful place in Brighton. Mum is in charge of the cleaning of all the royal and famous furniture and the rare and priceless carpets. She keeps everything fresh and free from moth-holes, and twice a year she washes all the china knick-knacks with her own hands, and she never breaks a thing!

'My Dad is Keeper of the Pavilion lights. He is the only person in Brighton who is allowed to touch the big glass candle-pieces in the ceilings. He changes all the electric bulbs, and when they have to be cleaned Dad personally unhooks the cut-glass drops. And he is the only one who knows how to put them back again without getting them mixed up! Even the Mayor of Brighton can't do that!'

He smiled proudly, for this was an oft-repeated part of the family saga, and the merman was impressed.

'Tell me about this Royal Pavilion,' he entreated. 'Describe those glass candle-pieces. I have never heard of such things before.'

And the boy who had spent much of his babyhood playing quietly on the Pavilion's floors, and whose earliest memories were of reaching up from his carrycot towards the pictured ceilings with their glittering chandeliers, described the place as if it had been his second home. He spoke of the music room with its delicate old instruments, and the kitchen with its iron-leaved palm-trees and illuminated turnspits. He told of nodding chinamen figures, the mock-bamboo furniture, the dolphin chairs and sofas and the lacquered cabinets. And the merman, who hardly understood a word of it, but was yet drunk with delight, nodded his head.

'It's all coloured,' the boy said, ' – just like a spilled paint-box!' And he lifted his hands and tilted them as if they too were spilling colours.

'Our Sea King has splendid halls,' said the merman. 'They are roped with pearls and spangled with doubloons. On our King's coral tables lie strange jewels and golden goblets from treasure chests, but they are paled by the green sea-light.'

'You should see the Pavilion when the Regency Exhibition is on!' the boy cried. 'They spread out gold plates and gold goblets and crystal glasses and everything glitters and flashes and shines.'

'Is it like when the sun falls on to the little waves?' asked the merman.

'Something like that,' the boy said. 'Not quite – but something.'

'I should like to see that Regency Exhibition,' said the merman.

So after that they often met at night-time on the beach. When they were sure of being undetected the merman would display his great tail for the boy's delight. He would splash it in and out of the sea: now it stood above the water with its enormous fins spread like fans, now falling as a tree-trunk it sent a spray of lighted bubbles to the moon. At last he would lash it to and fro in a froth of spray.

'That's great,' the boy would exclaim. 'That's *really* magnificent.'

'Tell me again about the cars,' the merman would plead. 'I want to understand – tell me about gears and petrol and licences and brakes and traffic regulations. Tell me again,' and the boy would repeat all he knew which really wasn't very much because he wasn't all that interested in motors. Nevertheless the merman sighed in admiration.

'How great and powerful are the brains of

earth-men that can understand those mysteries,' he said.

'I should like to ride in a car,' he went on dreamily. 'One day I was gazing through my glasses and I saw a mighty car. It was a shining purple colour, with silver fittings, and there were purple window blinds with silver fringes and people lined the street when it went by! Tell me about that splendid car.'

The boy began to laugh uncontrollably. He rolled helplessly upon the pebbles. At last he sat up, eyes streaming with mirth!

'Man, that was no ordinary car!' he gasped. 'That was the *posh hearse*. That was *the* posh hearse. And I know all about that because my uncle William drives it, and that's not often, for it's only used for rich folk's funerals! When my uncle drives that posh hearse he is dressed in black from head to toe from his shovver's hat to his toe-caps, and he don't look to right or left of him – just drives slow and steady and don't smile or look at anyone. My Mum says that takes a lot of doing because Uncle William is a laughing and friendly man.'

'What a great man your uncle must be!'

exclaimed the merman. 'I can think of nothing I would like better than to ride through the streets of your glittering town in such a grand vehicle as your uncle's posh hearse. Imagine riding in it all the way to your Royal Pavilion!'

The boy grinned. 'Only the rich and the dead can afford a ride in that,' he said. But the merman only smiled. Being an Immortal and having nothing under the sea with which to make comparison he did not understand the meaning of his friend's words.

On the dark nights when the mermaids swam in, the merman encouraged them to come further inshore, and to raise their voices so that the hidden boy could hear them conversing together. Once he managed to persuade them to sing some of their lovely sea-songs, knowing that this would please his friend most of all.

So beautiful and unexpected was that burst of mermaid singing that the night-life of busy Brighton stopped. Traffic halted, laughter was stilled and people crept from pubs and cafés and Bingo halls to stand and listen and wonder. The shipping as far as Shoreham Harbour came to a standstill as the glees, rounds and catches, the strange airs with delicate descants and the intricate plainsong of the sea, poured out from that dark beach. Only the dolphins in the underground Aquarium recognizing the sound dashed excitedly round their pool and cried out a shrill accompaniment.

At last, drunk with pleasure, the boy could contain himself no longer and springing to his feet he cried out for joy.

At once the mermaids were gone. A white-armed turn, a splash of tails and a foamy wake disappearing into blackness and it was over. Only their songs remained echoing in the ears and brain of the enchanted boy, who fell to his knees hugging himself and rocking to and fro as if to imprint each magical note upon every part and fibre of his recollection.

'One day,' he said at last, 'I will make songs like those. Though I don't think anyone on land could sing them as the mermaids do!'

'I swear that I heard the voices of dolphins,' said the merman. 'I have never known them to swim about these waters. They are the sea-folk's dearest pets and know our customs and our ancient songs.'

The boy explained about the tame dolphins and the sea-creatures who swam about the Aquarium and the merman made pained inquiries about the dolphins' welfare.

'Don't you worry about them, man,' said the boy. 'Those dolphins are very, very happy. Everyone pampers them and pets them and they just love their keepers. Do you know, their keepers kneel down and lean right over the pool and those old dolphins jump up and kiss them on the cheek they like them so much!

'I know about that because my cousin Stanley is one of the dolphin keepers and he is always talking about that.'

'Guardians of the Pavilion treasures, driver of the posh purple hearse, keeper of the Aquarium dolphins – what mighty and influential people your relatives are,' cried the merman, in an ecstasy of admiration.

And so the friendship progressed.

Then a time came when extra decorations were added to Brighton's decorative sea-front. Strings of bright pennants joined the coloured lights strung from the lamp-posts. White banners lettered in blue and gold were suspended from every pole and loudspeaker vans shouted from distant streets.

'The Regency Exhibition is opening soon,' said the boy. 'Famous actors and actresses will be dressed up to look like the old Prince Regent and his friends and my two little brothers are going to be pages with white wigs on their heads. And they're bringing gold and silver dishes in armoured cars to spread in the Pavilion dining-room!'

'My time along this coast will soon have run out,' said the merman. 'In a little while I will have to join the councillors of the deep sea for my term of office. I shall have so much to tell them, thanks to you, my kind friend. Could I have seen the Royal Pavilion before I departed my cup of happiness would have brimmed over. Still, I have seen the Brighton decorations and heard of the preparations for the Regency Exhibition, and what merman can boast of more than that?'

Hearing this the boy felt very sad. Somehow he had never thought a time would come when he would have to part from his friend, and he longed to make some wonderful final gesture to show how much the friendship had meant to him.

True to his promise, he had told no one of the mer-people's presence. None the less, knowing how the merman longed to see the splendours of the Royal Pavilion he had often pondered ways and means. Now he decided to speak to his wise Mum and ask her advice. 'Though I bet she won't believe me,' he thought.

But his Mum did believe him. When he took her aside at a quiet moment and blundered out his story she gave a ripe chuckle. She knew all about mer-people! There are hundreds along the coasts of her native land. Only of course in tropic waters the mer-people are a dark race. 'Coal black,' his mother said, 'and very, very friendly. Not at all afraid to show themselves and always ready to help the land-folk when they're in trouble!'

(And that's not as strange as you may think, because if you look around you in this country you'll find the odd old carving or sign that depicts a black merman or mermaid. The ancient sea-faring men must have met them on their voyages.)

Now the boy's Mum was a very kind woman and seeing how sad he was at the idea of parting from his friend, she said, 'Leave it to me,' and put her wits to work.

Presently she said, 'I think we could manage it, but it will mean speaking to your uncle William and your cousin Stanley, but I know they'll keep it secret. Uncle William because several of his family have been saved from drowning by helpful mer-people, and cousin Stanley because he daren't cross his Dad!

'It will have to be next Friday though — the night before the Exhibition opens. You just go down to the beach this evening and tell your friend to be *prepared for* anything on Friday night! Tell him I'll arrange something!'

When the boy told his friend the good news he was delighted. But then he groaned and shook his shaggy head. 'Alas, it is impossible,' he said, 'a trip like that would take time. I am afraid I would dry out long before we reached the Pavilion. Mer-people's tails are subject to dryness you know! Without moisture we suffer agonies and our scales drop off! In such a state of anguish as that I could never appreciate the beauties of your glorious Pavilion.'

'Mum knows all about mer-people and she says she'll arrange everything. She's a real good arranger so don't you worry,' said the boy firmly.

So Friday came at last. There was a high tide that night, and only a thin moon hovering behind fast-running clouds. The sea came in like oil and slopped against the sea wall. Brighton was so busy preparing for tomorrow's festivities that no one noticed a posh purple hearse parked up on the pavement outside the Aquarium's entrance. No one saw three dark figures, the boy's Dad, his uncle William and his cousin Stanley staggering up the steps with a large empty tank. Nor did anyone see how Uncle William, who was used to organizing the fitting-in of ornate coffins, directed the placing of that tank inside the purple hearse, nor how they drove off with it down to the front where the boy and the merman were waiting.

No inquisitive eye saw the filling of the tank,

bucket by bucketful from the ocean, no one heard the crunch of shingle as they raised and carried the merman across the beach and over to the hearse.

Cousin Stanley, handler of dolphins, knew just how the merman should be handled and took complete charge of the operation. Soon the happy sea-being sat waist-deep in water, gazing with joy from beneath the purple blinds as Uncle William started the engine. On one side of him sat his good friend the boy, on the other the boy's Dad and at the foot of the tank was Cousin Stanley ready to hold it steady as they turned the corners.

'At last, a dream come true!' cried the happy merman, and the three human faces opened in delighted smiles.

What a sight unfolded as the hearse moved slowly on its way. Uncle William took a roundabout route so that the merman could see as much of the town as possible. How he stared into the lit shop windows and marvelled at the articles that we find indispensable! How he trained his binoculars up to the rooftops and gasped at the traffic lights! Everything enchanted him. 'Oh what a tale I will have to tell my friends beneath the sea!' he said.

The hearse took a turn out of the shopping streets, and they passed light-festooned trees, many-coloured fountains and then – the Pavilion itself with its sea-green domes, came into view.

'Just as you described it! I should have known it anywhere!' said the merman fervently and he took the boy's hand between his great hard palms and squeezed it in gratitude.

Inside the Pavilion all was prepared. The turnstiles had been taken out and the boy's Mum had hunted in the Pavilion's lumber-room and found the old Prince Regent's own hip-bath. This was standing, ready-filled, just inside the entrance on a British Railway luggage trolley. (One of the boy's aunties' husbands was a porter at Brighton station.)

Seated in that gilded Regency bath (a sight in itself) the dazzled merman was wheeled slowly from room to room. At last he was to see all the curious and beautiful things his friend had told him about.

When the boy's father switched on the lights that illuminated the dazzling pendants the boy

nodded and his friend cried out with excitement, 'Yes, yes! Just as you said!'

Again and again the merman would beg to be allowed to stop at this or that splendid ornament so that he could store every detail in his memory, for the benefit of his friends below the sea.

In the great dining-room, rich and glittering with treasure, the boy's kind Mum unhooked a rope barrier so that the merman could lean forward between the chairbacks and touch the display of precious tableware, and feel the starched perfection of the white tablecloth. 'Just as you said!' he exclaimed again.

When they reached the music room he asked to be trundled forward so that he might touch the beautiful instruments, and when he saw the grand piano already open in anticipation of Sunday's concert, he knew what it was at once. 'Play it for me,' he entreated the boy. 'Let me hear some of that music you make in your head, so that I can hear it in my memory as I pass about the deep-sea caves performing my public duties.'

The boy looked at his Mum.

'*In for a penny; in for a pound* they say, don't they?' she said. So the boy sat down at the grand piano and played the songs from his head. First they were the mermaids' tunes, but presently little themes of his own crept into the sound and danced among the sea-rhythms and expanded until he turned it all into a gay dance-tune and Uncle William, Cousin Stanley, and the boy's Mum and Dad clapped softly to the rhythm, while the merman, tears of joy running down his cheeks, brought his own hard palms together.

But at last the boy's Mum said, 'Enough is enough, for time and tide wait for no man.' So he rose obediently from the piano stool, and took his turn to propel the trolley, where, comfortable in his Regency bath, the enraptured merman waited to be taken on the last lap of his journey.

Then it was all over! Outside the purple hearse awaited them. Under the practised supervision of Cousin Stanley the merman was again installed inside the Aquarium tank, and, waving and smiling to the boy's Mum, he was driven out of the gateway.

It was late now, and the streets were deserted. Uncle William drove swiftly round the square and down side streets and back to the sea-front. This was a new thrill for the merman who had never believed such speed possible. Holding fast to the sides of the tank, he raised himself high so that he might look over Uncle William's shoulders. It took all the efforts of the others to prevent him upsetting the tank in his excitement.

'Oh, you landsmen! What gods you are!' he cried.

But all too soon they reached the shore.

The tide had turned and gone a long way out, and they had to take several rests on the pebbles before they finally got the merman back to the sea, and even then, they had to wade in with him.

After a quick and refreshing dip he re-emerged to thank the three kind men and his friend the boy.

'Tomorrow,' he said, 'I shall be returning to the deep sea with many wonderful memories to share with my kinsfolk. But before I go, I should like to give my dear young friend a gift to keep always in memory of our friendship.'

From a deep pouch among his scales he produced a curious and curly shell – of a kind never seen before in all the land world.

'This shell holds all the sounds of the sea,' the merman said. 'When you come to make your music, put it to your ear sometimes to remind yourself of our mermaids and their songs.'

The boy was weeping at the thought that he would never see his friend again, but he put out his hand, and took the shell and raised it to his right ear. At once he began to smile. 'I hear the mermaids and the dolphins!' he cried, for it was indeed a curious and magic shell, rare even to the deep-sea dwellers.

'Farewell, then,' said the merman, raising his sturdy arm.

But 'Wait, wait!' cried the boy, 'I have something for you!' and he dived a hand down the neck of his pullover and took out a small parcel wrapped in snowy paper.

'Mum chose it,' he said. 'She said it would remind you of happy days and absent friends, and the sea will not harm it.'

Dawn was breaking and the gulls were stirring over the water, the first sunrays came through the running clouds as the merman opened his parcel, and exclaimed for joy.

There in his big hand lay a perfect china replica of the Royal Pavilion with the Brighton coat-of-arms painted on its courtyard and A PRESENT FROM BRIGHTON stamped across it in gold letters!

Too overcome for speech, the merman shook hands with Uncle William and Cousin Stanley and the boy's Dad. For a minute he rested a hand on the boy's head, then turning, he swam out to sea, one arm held high above his head clutching the Royal Pavilion aloft, so that it was the last thing they saw before he vanished from view.

And the boy, watching him go, raised the shell to his ear again, and had all the music of the sea to comfort him.

There are plenty of other mermen at Brighton, though I fancy they'll be too clever for you to spot. The mermaids come in now and again too when the nights are very dark. They have taken to sitting on the iron girders beneath the two piers combing their thick tresses and whispering together. You may hear them whisper-whisper-whispering at night if you go out on the pier and put your ear down against one of the cracks in the decking.

Or, if you need further evidence, I suggest you look at those iron girders some time. You'll see whole bundles of mermaid's hair caught up on the struts. Mermaids are very careless about their combings!

6

The Magic Badge

ONCE upon a time there were five children who lived with their Mum and Dad and Gran and Granddad in a funny little house with no front garden, and a yard at the back.

What a squeeze it was!

Gran and Granddad had the big front bedroom.

Mum and Dad had the little back bedroom.

Clint and Andy and Tiny-boy slept in the middle bedroom.

As for Lulu and Emma-Linda, they slept on a put-you-up in the downstairs front room.

And all the family ate together in the back kitchen, and what a squeeze *that* was!

As they hadn't got a bathroom they had to bathe in the back scullery – and they could only do that at night-time, because that was where the gas-stove was and someone was always wanting to boil a kettle or cook things or wash something during the day.

So every night there was always someone having a bath in the back scullery, and when I tell you that as well as the bath and the gas-stove there was a refrigerator, a washing-machine, Dad's moped, and Tiny-boy's push-chair there as well, you will agree that that was a squeeze too.

Still, they were all very happy, Mum, Dad, Gran, Granddad, Clint, Andy, Lulu and Emma-Linda; Tiny-boy too, and the cat – he was happy because though it was a tight squeeze in that little house, no one ever trod on him, and everybody loved him.

Even so, there were times when they all agreed that it would be nice to have a bit more room. 'Still,' they all said, 'still – we've got each other!'

Now Andy, the eldest boy, belonged to a gang and all the boys in his gang wore badges. They wore them all over the front of their pullovers and jackets. All sorts of badges, every colour and size. Some with pictures on them, some with writing. Round badges like buttons, square ones and shaped ones; army badges too if you were lucky.

The Magic Badge

Andy had quite a few badges but his friend Les had dozens. Les hadn't any brothers and sisters, but his parents gave him lots of pocket-money, so where Andy could only swop with boys outside the gang for a badge he hadn't got, Les could buy them.

It wasn't really surprising then that when Andy happened to be coming home from school one day and saw a badge lying on the pavement at the top of his road he should stoop and pick it up.

'Cor,' Andy said, 'what a smasher.'

It certainly was! It flashed and shone as he turned it about in the sunshine and looked, as Andy said, 'Golder than gold.'

There was a pin on the back of it and writing on the front. Andy didn't like reading very much, so he didn't bother to read the writing. He opened the pin, and stuck it through his jersey and snapped it shut again – and there he was – with the badge glittering and glimmering on his front.

It was his sister Lulu who read the writing. She was a great one for reading everything she set eyes on – not only books and comics but road-signs and hoardings and notices of all kinds.

'What a funny badge,' she said. 'It says "Kick me".'

'Well, if that's what you want,' she said, and kicked him – not too hard – on the leg.

'Ha-ha "Kick me",' shouted Emma-Linda. 'Certainly!' and she kicked him, *rather* hard, on the other leg.

'Do you want to be kicked then?' said Clint, who was a big strong boy, though he wasn't as old as Andy.

But Andy dodged round the table and said, 'Lay off.'

'You don't want to wear a badge like that,' his Mum said. 'You'll be asking for trouble.'

'You'll be black and blue in no time,' said his Gran.

'I expect that's why you found it. Someone got tired of wearing it and being kicked about,' said Emma-Linda. 'It had been thrown away. Not lost.'

'It's such a nice badge,' said Andy sadly. 'Still, I don't want to be kicked,' he said, and took it off.

He put the badge in his pocket and once or twice that day he took it out and looked at it. 'KICK ME' – that's what those letters said. 'K-i-c-k m-e' he spelled it out to himself to make sure.

Suddenly Andy felt angry. It was just his luck to have found such a special-looking badge and then be unable to wear it after all. Even Les hadn't got one that shone like that.

'All right – "kick me" it is!' he said, and he

tossed the glittering badge into the air and as it fell he caught it on the toe of his shoe and kicked it up and away over the backyard fence. 'Goal!' he shouted.

Then he went indoors to have his tea.

'Oh dear,' said Mum who was just bringing in a dish of baked beans. 'You children grow and grow. I can hardly get round the table for you.'

'I wish we had a bit more room,' said Dad.

'I wish we had a great big house with a bath-room, and a bedroom each, and a garden and a shed for Granddad to do his woodwork in,' said Lulu.

'And a room where Tiny-boy could have a playpen,' said Emma-Linda.

'I wish we could have a real dining-room like the one they had where I was a girl in service,' said Gran, 'with a sideboard and a chiffonier and room to seat twenty.'

This was a favourite game with that family – wishing for a big house with lots of rooms in it. No one really meant it. Andy usually joined in too, but today he was fed up and cross.

'I wish you could all have what you wish for,

and then we might have some peace,' he said rudely.

'And wishing's as far as we'll get,' said Mum, helping Tiny-boy to a sausage, and Dad and Granddad began to laugh.

But then they stopped. Everyone stopped. They stopped talking and eating and laughing and wishing. Because suddenly, there they were – in the dining-room, Gran's dining-room – the one she was always on about.

They were sitting spaced out round a long table. A posh table with a lace cloth running down the middle of it, and their tea – the baked beans and sausages, the loaf and Mum's home-made cake served up on silver dishes, and everyone's mugs and cups turned to see-through china with roses painted on it!

There was the sideboard and the chiffonier – just as Gran had described them. In fact – there they were, in the big house they were always talking about and all the things they'd ever wished for were in it too!

Although they didn't know it – it had come about because Andy had done what the badge asked – he'd kicked it – and as it was a magic one and he had wished (even though he had wished rudely) everyone's wishes had come true at once.

'It's magic,' said Gran.

'It's luck,' said Granddad.

'It's like winning the pools and not having to wait to spend the money,' said Dad, after they had been all over the new house and garden and marvelled at its wonders.

'I can't wait to get at those tools in the shed,' Granddad said happily.

'My bedroom is just like the telly,' said Lulu. 'I can't wait to get into that satin bed!'

'We should be happy as kings here,' exclaimed Mum as she put Tiny-boy into the playpen on the floor of his special play-room. 'Even Pussy – did you see the lovely cat-basket in the kitchen?'

And at first they *were* happy. For as well as the fine house, the magic wish had spread itself in many directions. For one thing there were so many gadgets Mum and Gran had hardly any cleaning to do. There were so many toys the children were always finding new ones they hadn't noticed before. And Dad and Granddad didn't have to go out to work any more because every Thursday morning a registered letter came through the post with five hundred pound notes in it, which was much, much more than they needed. In fact, after a while they didn't bother to open the envelope – they just threw it into a big oak chest on the top landing as it was – that's how rich they were!

But would you believe it? After a time they stopped being happy.

Every night Mum went to her splendid bedroom.

Every night Dad went to his splendid bedroom.

So did Gran, and Granddad, Clint, Andy and Lulu.

Emma-Linda didn't go straight to bed though. Poor Tiny-boy cried so much in his splendid and lonely room she went and fetched him and took him into her bed every night.

Each day they sat around the enormous table in their big dining-room where there was plenty of room for everyone to sit in comfort and lots of room for Mum to move about.

But they weren't a bit happy.

'I don't know why it is,' Dad said one day, 'but I feel FED UP.'

'That's funny,' said Mum coming in at that moment from her wonderful modern kitchen, 'so do I.'

'I've got the hump,' said Gran sadly, 'and so's Granddad – look at him.'

Everyone looked at Granddad. Then everyone said, 'I'm fed up too.'

'It's all this poshness. It's boring,' said Emma-Linda.

'Perhaps we'd be better if we had a holiday,' said Mum.

'That's it – we need a change,' said Granddad, perking up at the thought.

'We need to rough it a bit,' said Dad.

Everyone was quiet for a while, then Dad said, 'Got it!'

'Mum, start packing up a few bits and pieces,' he said, 'I won't be long.'

He winked at Granddad and was off.

They began to pack at once and it was as well they did, for in no time at all, back came Dad, driving a car, and behind the car, on tow, was a caravan.

'In you get,' he said. 'We're off for a holiday.'

And off they all went, through the town and

out into the country, up hills and down valleys and on to the sea. Back from the sea and off along the motorway to the mountains. Day after day they travelled and camped.

What a squeeze it was!

Gran and Granddad had the big bunk-bed in the living-room part of the caravan. Mum and Dad had the small bunk-bed in the kitchen part of the caravan. Lulu and Emma-Linda had the bed with the roof-you-push-up on the top of the caravan, and Clint and Andy slept in a tent outside. As for Tiny-boy, sometimes he slept with the girls, sometimes with the boys. He didn't mind which. And the cat? He slept on the back window-ledge of the caravan all day and at night-time he prowled about looking for field-mice.

When the weather was fine they ate their meals outside. When it wasn't they crowded into the living-space in the caravan, and that was a very tight squeeze indeed for all of them – in fact, Tiny-boy had to sit in the sink and Emma-Linda on the window-sill by Pussy.

Still, they were happy as the day was long.

'This is the life, eh, Mum?' said Dad.

'You're right there, Dad,' Mum replied.

'We won't go back to that house any more, will we?' asked Gran.

'It was too lonely – all that space,' said Granddad.

So they decided to live in the caravan for ever and ever, spring, summer, autumn and winter, wandering and camping on an endless holiday.

That *was* the life all right.

But it could be altered at any time – it just depends on Emma-Linda though she doesn't know it, and nor does the family. I'll tell you why:

One day, when they were sitting round their camp-fire, brown as gypsies, eating their baked beans and sausages, Emma-Linda happened to rub her hand across a patch of moss.

Under her fingers she felt something hard.

She picked it up and looked at it. It was a shining gold badge with writing on it.

Emma-Linda had by now been away from school for so long she had forgotten all the letters she had ever learned. But she remembered the badge Andy had found and wasn't taking any chances.

No one had noticed her or seen what she was looking at. So, very quietly, Emma-Linda scratched a hole in the ground, put the badge in it, and covered it with loose earth.

'No one's going to kick *me*,' she thought.

It was a pity she hadn't kept up her reading. Do you know why?

It didn't say, '*kick* me' on that badge at all.

It said, 'BURY me.'

So, at any moment . . .

7

The Little Chap

IT was about the time when the papers were full of stories about mysterious flying objects passing across the sky and when even the children were talking about Martians and Moon-men. It was that time when we spent the year at Gran's.

Because she didn't know what to do with us at times Gran would send us on errands. This time it was across the heath and up to the beekeeper's to buy honey for Sunday tea.

All the way there, our Alan played Martians fighting space-monsters, or said, 'What would you do if – ?' without waiting for an answer. Just giving me his ideas and kicking up clouds of the chalky sand whenever a patch occurred across the path, and pretending to fight off strange beasts with the sappy fronds of young bracken.

He was still talking about Beings from Space when we got to the beekeeper's, way out on the heath, under the pine knoll.

The Little Chap

He was a very old man, that beekeeper. His hands were twisted and he lifted down our pot of honey with the pads of his fingers, then hooked a little finger under one side of his steel glasses to adjust them so that he could see us better.

Young Alan went on with his space-talk.

'Flying saucers and Beings from another world. That's what they're saying nowadays, is it? Well, I'm not surprised. Not at all,' said the old, old man.

He looked across the heath, where the bees were bumbling in the purple and gold of warm ling and gorse blossoms. 'Don't say it's nonsense, Missy. Say you don't know. Ay, say you don't know.

'There are things you stumble on in the lonely parts. Take what we used to call fairy-rings when I was a lad. Round as a parlour table-top and the harebells laid flat like they had been trod and trod. Out on the heath time and again you'd come upon them. Fairy trod they used to say.' He paused and peered for a moment from under his raggedy white eyebrows. Then, seeing that we children were attentive, he went on in a seemingly irrelevant way, as if caught up in an old memory:

'We never had children of our own,' he said, 'though we should have liked them. Especially Mother because she came of a large family and the heath is a lonely place for one as is used to company. Still for all that, we once had a dear little chap who gave us a deal of joy – a deal of joy.'

He paused and smiled at us, showing strong old yellow teeth below the fringe of his grey moustache.

'We were passing middle age then, and I was still working as head cowman down at Long's Bottom, and Mother was becoming fretting lonely. It was dull for her then, with me away all day, especially with her legs going sudden like they did. She never moped to me, that wasn't her way; but I knew for all that.

'Well, it were one evening when I was coming home – 'bout this time of year I reckon – that I found this little chap walking all alone in the heather.'

He paused and stared suddenly at my brother who was trapped by his gaze:

'Stark naked he was, with h'eyes like black-berries and brown all over as if clothes had never covered him, and a bare little head with never a hair on it, shining like a h'acorn. There he was, chit-chattering to himself in a foreign sort of language that sounded low and tinkly like a bunch of harebells does when you shakes it close by your ear.'

Alan and I nodded, we knew that sound from past experiment.

'I took his little hard hand in mine, and asked him kind where he had come from, but he only smiled at me. So I looked round for his kin and hollered a bit, thinking at first he might be a tinker's chavvi, but the heath was bare of people. So I took him home to Mother.'

He paused again and I knew our Alan's mind was making pictures like the ones my mind was making – flashes of shiny brown skin and hare-bells and blackberry eyes.

'I knew we should have given him up to someone,' the old man told us; 'but Mother said "no". The minute she clapped eyes upon his little merry face she knew he was hers for as long as he could be spared to us.

'Mother took him straight indoors and he went happy, holding to the side of her h'apron because she hadn't a hand to spare along of her sticks. And somehow she managed to bath him in the old washtub as I filled, and dried him and covered him with one of my h'old night-shirts and fed him, and put him to sleep at last on the ottoman beside our bed.

'That evening she set to work with the sewing

machine making oddments of clothes for him.

' "Bill," she said, "we'll watch the papers and we'll keep our ears open, and if he's got worried parents we'll send him back good and honest. But it seems to me," she says, "as no mortal woman on earth would let a little chap like that wander about the heath on his own so dis-respectable with no clothes on."

'So we kep' him, for no one ever came inquiring for him and we never heard of such as he being given out lost. As the months went by we came near to forgetting that he wasn't our very own.'

He paused again and we watched the bees in the hardy garden flowers as they dipped and dived, clambered and clung and emerged yellow dusted and nectar dizzy!

'He was a queer little fellow was that, but very good and gay. He was keen, too, and quick to show how fond he was by helping us best he could, for all he would never turn his tongue to speak our language. His little nimble fingers were all about the garden pulling weeds for me, and it seemed wherever his fingers fell the flowers have growed the better for it.

'It was the same in the house with Mother. He would fix his bright little eyes on her face, and then do for her the very thing she was just about to do for herself. Many's the morning I'd come down to find him up and about in the chilly first dawn, pulling in firewood with his little thin arms, all the time chuckling to himself as if he was having the time of his life.'

Oh, I saw it all – beyond the golden globes of honey-light, beyond the stretches of sun-drenched heath, that strange and happy honey-brown face full of smiles and blessings.

'Mother called him Billy after me and he seemed to know his name, for he would sort of come fluttering down the stairs or across the garden when we called him, quick and pretty as a bird. No one never did know how old he was, but if cleverness was anything he was old as the hills.

'Well, things were very happy for us all. For two years Billy was Mother's own dear little chap. He never once seemed to pine for those he must have known before we took him in. He might have been our very own. And loving! The love in him was so strong it seemed to fill the whole place. Especially towards the end.

'It was in the third summer I noticed a change in the little chap. I never marked its beginning, but his movements became less quick and his smiles less bright, and sometimes, instead of helping us like he'd done before he'd go out into the garden and sit very quiet watching them old spiders making their webs in the currant bushes.

'I didn't like to say anything to Mother, but she noticed all right, for one day she said, "Bill — something funny keeps happening up in Billy's bedroom." We'd given him the little apple-loft under the roof where the martins nested, and hard though it'd been for her, Mother had climbed to keep it sweet for him every day he was with us. "I've been finding long threads of a sort of silky stuff all over the place — like the beginnings of cobwebs — only stronger — and prettier. I brush them away each morning, but they are back again next day."

' "Some game he's playing with your work-box," I says, though I knew our Billy never played games.

' "Bill," she says, "I've no thread in my work-box as pretty as that. And another thing,

Father, Billy's altering. He don't like me bathing him no more. He goes off and hides when he sees me put the big saucepans on the stove. He don't like to be seen naked no more."

'It seemed she was afeared to tell me at first, in case I took against the little chap, but now it all poured out and with the telling came her poor tears.

' "Bill, I think there's something queer growing on his chest. He won't let me look. He laughs, but he won't let me. He's grown different," Mother says.

'And all this time Billy was growing stiller and quieter. Not ill, but quiet as if he had a deal to ponder on, and graver too and somehow powerful. I suppose we had always known he was uncommon. Unchancey really. But we just loved him still and let him be.

'So in a way we were prepared when one Saturday afternoon he turns away from us, and climbs up to his little room, very slow and tired-like in the little shirt and breeches Mother had sewn for him, with his little bald head bent low as he went. But not as if he had a sickness, mind – but tired – tired out. When Mother gathered her sticks and made to follow him, he turned and shook his head at her and went up alone as if he knew what he had to do.

' "Leave him be," I said to her. "He's tired, the dear chap. Leave him be till the morning," I told her.

'But there was no comfort in Mother. "No, Father," she said (did I tell you we'd started calling each other "Mother" and "Father" since Billy came?) "No, Father, we must just be thankful They let us have him this long. For you know, Bill, he's not of our sort."

'Next morning I helped her up the steps and we went together into Billy's room, timid as children – not knowing what to expect, but somehow knowing that things would be strange.'

The old man paused, and looked deeply, first into my face and then into our Alan's – and I saw that his eyes were full of old man's tears.

'Billy wasn't there. Not our little chap. Not any more. But all across that little room, from ceiling to bed-knob, from quilt to wash-stand, from beam to floorboard was a great shiny cradle of silky threads, and high up to its middle, rolled up in a bundle of shining silk, still winding and weaving, like I've seen a silkworm wind and weave was a Creature that must once have been our Billy.

'No, Missy, 'twern't terrible. 'Twere a beautiful and a wonderful sight. We stared as if we were peering through the gate of Paradise, wonderstruck and happy.

' "Come away, Father," says Mother at last, with the tears dropping from her eyes because it was so wonderful and yet so pitiful for her. "We must just wait for what comes of it. But oh, Bill," she says, "I fear that what comes won't be for us."

'So we left it alone until a time came when the threads stopped spinning and the great silky ball lay still in its cradle. Which was the twenty-first day after our Billy had vanished.

'It was late afternoon, and I'd just come in, when we heard a busy sound – like the snapping of bands, and we hurried upstairs together – and as God judges all – Mother went forgetful of her bad legs – without stick or crutch, carried by the wonder of it! And both of us so full of love for our Billy as not to be afraid.

'Just as we were entering that little attic room, the last threads went, and we saw the beautiful shining bundle fall apart. And out of it came a creature of glory. Smaller than ever Billy had been but shining like a light. It had sort of wings that trembled and shook, and opened and grew, so fast and strange they were like wings on wings.

'It had clusters of eyes opening out on the sides of its head like bubbles of soap, and feelers like the bees have – only longer and curly-looking.

'It was a lovely and lovable thing.

' "Billy," says Mother and puts out her arms to it. But it wasn't Billy no more.

' "We have to let it go," I said, for I saw that those lovely wings were meant for a wider sky than the sky of our poor world. Mother saw that too.

' "Open the window, Father," she said. "But follow him, follow him, Bill. I'd do it myself but for my legs. Follow and see that nothing harms him."

'For to her, even then, he was still in part the little chap she had loved and looked after.

'Then this lovely thing seemed to look at her, with all them bright and shining eyes, and goodness seemed to pour from that looking like the scent comes from the trumpets of lilies.

'Then, it shook out its new wings, and sailed out of the window.

'I hurried downstairs and watched it for a while, hovering over the garden and the hives, and then it bore off gently to the open heath, and although the sun was setting it seemed like the creature held its own light, pure and steady against it.

'I followed after as best I could, until it was lost to sight behind the trees.

'I never saw that lovely thing again. I saw something else though.

'Flying saucers you was saying? Well, I don't know. They may call it that. Anyway I saw it – just above the place where I'd first found him. Mind – it was darkish by then but there was light enough to see it rising, round and flattish and spinning with a noise like an 'umming top makes as it went up and away. Yes, you could say saucerish.

'I stayed there until the moon came up,

staring and hoping for more wonders, but all I saw was a round fairy-ring mark in the turf before me where that round thing had been.

'No, I h'aint seen nothing since. And you never hear of fairy-rings being found hereabouts these days so I take it they don't favour these parts no more.'

'What do you think?' whispered our Alan, his eyes popping like blue grapes.

'What do I think Billy was? Well, I thought maybe a fairyman but Mother said he was a Seraphim – like in the Bible because of his wings on wings and his loving ways. Anyway he wasn't of this world. I suppose nowadays they'd call him a creature from Mars or some-such.'

I whispered a question.

'The silky threads? Ah yes. Mother gathered them up and joined them, and in the winter evenings before her hands got bad she crocheted them into a great shawl for herself to wear round her poor shoulders.

'She loved it so much, that when she went, I had it put in with her, wrapped round her. It was a lovely sight. In the coffin, as she lay there, you might have fancied she were covered in folded wings.'

And saying this, the old man put the jar of honey into my hands, and forgetting the silver coin on the bench outside his door, turned and went within, and left us to wander trailing glorious dreams of colour across the heath and back to our Gran's – with only a pot of honey to show for our afternoon.

8

The Old White Ghost and the Old Grey Granddad

THERE was once an old white ghost who lived behind a water-pipe in an old-fashioned scullery in an old, old house. In this scullery was a big stone sink and a great copper boiler for washing clothes.

For many years this old white ghost haunted the scullery. He made terrible noises in the water-pipes, and after dark, when someone came downstairs to iron the clothes by candlelight he would slip inside the clothes basket and ruffle the washing and then shoot up suddenly in a sheet, or creep across the floor in an old black sock.

Some nights he would blow feathers from the pillow-slips in front of the candle to make strange shadows on the wall; and sometimes – sometimes he would drip a cold-water drop on the neck of the person who was ironing. One cold drop. Aaaah!

AND THEN HE'D BLOW THE CANDLE
OUT. OOOOH!

People hated his tricks. They became very
frightened. Soon they refused to go into the
scullery at all.

They stopped using it for washing, and over
the years it got filled up with all the things no
one wanted to throw away.

At last a very large family came to live in that

old house. There was a father and mother and their seven children and an old grey granddad. Now there was a battered pram and an old push-bike, an old clothes wringer with wooden rollers for crushing water out of the washing, and several old tubs, and a great bundle of comics on the scullery floor. In the stone sink stood a pile of old gramophone records and an old-fashioned gramophone with a tin horn and a handle to wind it up with. Perched on top of the copper was an old basket-chair. And over and under and between all these things were broken toys and rags and rubbish.

The mother took all her washing to the launderette up the road, and as all her family wore drip-dry clothes no ironing was needed. So nobody ever went into the scullery.

All these things that nobody wanted got dustier and dustier, under a great grey cobweb blanket.

At night the old white ghost came out from behind the water-pipe and made ghostly noises. He moaned and sighed until the cobwebs rocked and shivered and the basket-chair creaked. But there was no one to hear him. No one to tremble with fear or run away shrieking. 'I might as well not bother,' the old white ghost said mournfully.

One reason why no one heard him was because there were so many noises in the house anyway. The family never stopped making noises of one kind or another: shouting, hammering, sawing, sewing-machining, vacuuming, and quarrelling. And the radio, TV, and hi-fi were always switched on, all at the same time.

Only the old grey granddad was quiet. He sat in a chair in the corner of the sitting-room, with his hands over his ears to keep out the din.

One day this old grey granddad felt he couldn't stand the racket any longer, so he got out of his chair and began to prowl about the house. Every room was filled with people, their things, and their noise!

'If only I could find somewhere quiet,' the poor old man said. 'If only I could find a quiet place for myself.'

At last he crept down the kitchen steps and found himself in the scullery. The spiders had woven so many webs that only a dim light crept through the window, but the old man peered around in the gloom and took a fancy to what he saw.

'Why,' he said, 'I could make myself a snug little place down here. I could get them upstairs to help me clear out the rubbish, and, with a lick of whitewash here and a dab of paint there it would come up a treat!

'After all,' said the old grey granddad, 'I more than pay my way so they owe me something!'

And all the time he stood there, talking to himself, the old white ghost watched him from behind the water-pipe in the corner. The old white ghost was interested, but he didn't show himself, he just waited and bided his time.

The old grey granddad went back upstairs and he began to shout – louder than the loudest child to make himself heard.

'I pay my way,' he yelled, 'so I've got my rights. I want that scullery downstairs for my own private place and I'd thank you all to help me clear it out and make it homelike.'

And because his family were very fond of him, and because they knew he had justice on his side, they all stopped their hammering, banging, sawing, machining, shouting and making all the other noises, and got together to clear out the old-fashioned scullery.

What a time they had – carrying all the old things out into the yard and stacking them up by the dustbins!

Sometimes the old grey granddad would shout, 'Not that! Not that! I could do with that.'

In that way he saved the basket-chair for himself. He got the two youngest children scrubbing it clean, and the mother upstairs looking out a cushion for it. 'I always liked to sit in a basket-chair,' the old grey granddad said.

He found an old folding-table behind the wringer, and enough planks of wood to make himself some shelves – as for the old gramophone with the tin horn – he went mad with joy when that turned up, and he looked at the pile of records. 'All those old songs – all those old bands!' he said. 'They don't make music like that nowadays. I can listen to my heart's content.'

And when they began to clear out the bundles of old comics he said, 'Weary Willie and Tired Tim! Why that takes me back to my boyhood! They'll be just the thing for me to read when

I'm sitting in my basket-chair with my table at my elbow.'

And all this time the old white ghost made never a sound nor a movement, he just watched from behind the water-pipe. He watched while they cleared the scullery. He watched while they whitewashed and painted and hung shelves. He watched while the father laid a carpet that the mother had found in a second-hand shop. He watched and waited until at last the old grey granddad was alone in his nice new quarters. Until he was sitting in his basket-chair with his pile of old comics on the table and the freshly oiled gramophone and the well-dusted records to hand in the nicely scrubbed sink.

He waited till the old man had switched on the electric lamp that the father had wired for him, and spread out his toes to the electric fire the eldest grandson had fixed in place of the old copper-fire, and reached for the first copy of *Chips* before 'Uuuggh – Ah-h-h-h,' he said in the water-pipe. 'Uh, uh, uh, uh!'

He looked hard at the old grey granddad, but the old man didn't stir. After all the family racket he'd put up with for so long, he wasn't to be upset by ghostly water-pipes. Instead, he smiled sweetly, and leaning forward, he wound the handle of the gramophone, and the scullery was full of the gay and scratchy sound of a long-ago band of the Grenadier Guards. It was as if the ghosts of the old dead bandsmen filled the little warm scullery as they listened to their music. The old granddad welcomed them with pleasure.

The old white ghost was puzzled.

Presently, however, he grew bold again, and he began to rustle the pile of comics, but the old grey granddad didn't seem to mind a bit. He just picked up a big flat-iron that he was using for a door-stop and put it on top of the pile. 'Draughts,' he said.

The old white ghost remembered his trick with the water, and loosed a drop on the old granddad's neck. 'Condensation,' said that happy old man. 'It's the old pipes warming up.'

The old white ghost tried to blow out the light, as he'd blown out candles in the old haunting days. But the electric bulb never flickered, and the old grey granddad went on to read *Comic Cuts*.

The old white ghost was baffled. He began to moan from sheer despair. 'I want to haunt you,' he said. 'Please let me frighten you.'

The old grey granddad looked up over his spectacles and saw the flickering outline of the old white ghost. 'It's no good,' he said, 'I know all about you. Everyone knows about you. You think you're a ghastly spectre and so did a lot of other people. I know you're just draught, and air-locks in the pipes, and condensation – I know you can be mice or rats or imagination, so don't ask me to be afraid of you.

'I tell you what,' said the old grey granddad, 'there's an old stool over in the corner, I'll bring it up near to the fire here, and you can sit your-self down beside me and listen to the music. You can take a peek over my shoulder at these comics, they're good for a laugh any time. In that way – I won't worry you and you won't worry me.'

And that's just what the old white ghost did. He perched himself on the stool and listened to the long-dead voices of comic singers and mournful singers, and the long-lost strains of forgotten bands. Sometimes he took a peek

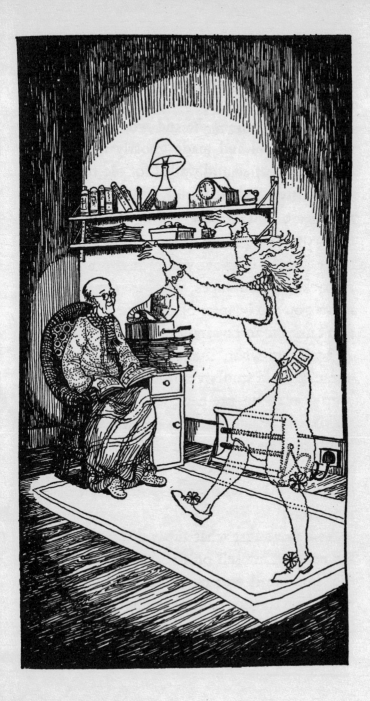

over the old granddad's shoulder and they laughed together over old jokes.

And if sometimes the old white ghost got up from his stool and made ghostly noises in the pipes, or moaned and wailed for old times' sake, the old grey granddad only said: 'Ah – but if it's real noise you're after – that lot upstairs can beat you hollow!'

9

The Old Woman who Lived in a Real Glass Vinegar Bottle

DON'T you let anyone tell you that it wasn't really a glass bottle – that it was really made of leather, or that it was a wooden cask, or, come to that a Kentish oast-house. No, it was a bottle all right.

The old woman in the story lived in a great green-glass bottle, shaped like those carboys people make gardens in, only much bigger of course. It lay on its side in an untidy yard full of wooden boxes and fish-scales behind a fish-and-chip shop.

The man who owned the fish-and-chip shop was always running out of vinegar, because his customers liked to drench their chips in it before they took them home. He once saw these great bottles full of vinegar advertised in a trade journal and had been tempted to send for one. The trouble was that when it was finally empty the dustmen refused to take it away, so he was quite glad to let the old woman make a home in it. In exchange she cleaned out the shop in the mornings.

Anyway, it *was* a real glass bottle, though some of the story got a bit mixed up by the time it reached the story books.

As you know, at first the old woman was perfectly happy in her vinegar bottle. She was proud of it. She kept it beautifully polished and made curtains to keep out the rude stares of the neighbours; she nailed together some of the wooden fish-boxes and made a flight of steps up to her front door (which was the screw-top of the vinegar bottle, mounted on wood, with a fancy brass knocker-cum-letter-box cut into it), and put pots of geraniums on each step.

In fact, the old woman managed very nicely on her pension, and the left-over fish-and-chips that the shopkeeper let her take home. (This was a good arrangement as she had no means of cooking in the vinegar bottle.) Once a week she went to play Bingo in a hall that used to be a cinema. This hall belonged to a cousin of the fish-and-chip-shop owner, so she got in half-price as a friend of the family. All in all, it was a happy life.

Then, one day when she was going down to the town to draw her pension money a strange thing happened. She was taking her usual short-cut which was an alley between two warehouses, when she heard a noise coming out of the drain in the gutter that ran down the middle. It was a loud croaking noise with a kind of gasp in it, that sounded like 'HELP, HELP!'

So of course the old woman stopped and looked down the drain. And there, staring up at her with eyes like saucers and its big mouth trembling with woe was a great yellow toad.

'Let me out. Please, let me out,' said the toad.

'What did you want to get in for?' said the old woman who lived in a glass vinegar bottle.

'I didn't want to. I was thrown in. I was thrown in by a bad boy who put the top on so that I couldn't get out,' said the toad sadly. 'I live under the manhole on the corner over there. Please let me out. My family will be wondering what has become of me.'

So the old woman crooked the handle of her

umbrella through the bars of the drain-top, gave a pull, and off it came, and the yellow toad jumped out.

For a moment he stood, blowing his throat in and out in the way toads do, and then he said, 'You've saved my life, old woman.'

'That's all right. Don't mention it,' she said kindly.

'No, no,' cried the toad. 'You deserve a

reward. Now, we toads have certain powers — we can with great effort, grant the occasional wish. After what you've done for me I'd be delighted to make such an effort on your behalf. Is there anything you'd like to ask for?'

Now the old woman had heard about people making hasty magic wishes, and she'd always thought if she'd ever had the chance to make one she'd think carefully first, so she said, 'Well, not at the moment. Could I take my time?'

'Certainly,' replied the toad. 'Just turn it over in your mind, and when you are ready to wish, come and knock on my front door and I'd be delighted to oblige you.' And off he hopped to the manhole cover, and it lifted and he went inside and was gone.

All the way to and from the post office the old woman thought, but she didn't know what to wish for.

It wasn't till the evening, when she was gazing through the green-glass window of her vinegar bottle that she knew what to ask for. Just beyond the fish-and-chip shop was a block of new council flats. She could see every window gleaming in the evening sunshine.

'The lucky folk who get one of those won't have to look through green bottle-glass,' she said to herself. 'They will have bathrooms with hot and cold water, and kitchens with cookers and fridges and balconies with flowers on, and if they are lucky enough to live up high they'll have a lift to travel up and down in! I could do worse than wish for one of those!'

So, instead of going to bed, the old woman kicked off her slippers and put on her shoes and went off down to the manhole on the corner of the alley and knocked hard.

Out came the toad at once looking very pleased to see her and to listen to her wish. 'I think that can be managed,' he said kindly and he rolled his great eyes until they spun like Catherine-wheels and made some magic sounds in his pulsing throat.

'Go home and see what's what,' he said when he had finished.

So the old woman went home. As soon as she got there she knew that something had happened. In the street that ran behind the fish-and-chip shop stood a green mini-car, and standing by it was the council's chief housing officer. She knew him at once. Everyone did – his photograph was always appearing in the local paper.

'Ah, just the lady,' he said with a smile. 'This is your day, madam. The council have, by unanimous vote, allotted you first pick of one of our new council flats. We feel that anyone who could keep a vinegar bottle so spick and span will make an ideal tenant, and set a good example to the others.'

So the old woman moved into the new block of flats at once. She picked the highest one of all. It had a wonderful view of the town and its balcony had tubs of mixed flowers on it. And there was a lift to take her up and down to it and a lift-man to touch his cap to her. For a while she was as happy as a queen.

She still cleaned the fish-and-chip shop every morning and collected the left-over fish-and-chips for her dinner. But now she could warm them up in the oven in her new kitchen, and eat them while she admired the view from her high windows. She still had her pension and her weekly Bingo – who could want more?

As for the vinegar bottle, she forgot all about it, and it grew dirty and dusty, its inside became misted over with condensation and the geraniums withered and died. It was no longer a home – but just an old bottle that the dustmen wouldn't take away.

One day when the old woman was washing the fish-fryer in the shop she heard the owner talking on the telephone:

'Oh yes,' he said, 'a lovely villa down near the river. Six bedrooms with showers, a modern kitchen *and* a swimming-pool! All fully furnished and a coloured TV too.'

The old-woman-who-used-to-live-in-the glass-vinegar-bottle lifted her head and listened. In her mind's eye she seemed to see that villa.

' – and an annual sum of five thousand pounds for its upkeep,' said the fish-shopman. 'Oh yes, there's a lucky person about somewhere.' And he laughed and rang off.

The old woman went back to her council flat with her mind in a turmoil. Why on earth hadn't she asked for a place like that when the toad had given her a wish? A swimming pool and all those bedrooms, and a coloured television set!

That night was Bingo night, and all the way

down to the hall-that-used-to-be-a-cinema she was saying, 'I must have been mad.'

She took the usual short cut through the alley. When she arrived at the manhole she stopped. 'Why not? I can only try,' she said to herself. 'After all, maybe I was going to be given that flat anyway. Perhaps I've still got a wish to come.'

She knocked hard and at once the cover was raised and the yellow toad hopped out. He looked delighted to see her. 'It was kind of you to call to thank me,' he said. 'Some people never bother.'

The old woman looked rather guilty. But she said, 'Oh yes, of course, thank you very much. Only – ' she said, 'I was wondering if perhaps you could change my wish a bit – ' and she quickly told the yellow toad about the villa the shopkeeper had been talking about on the telephone.

The toad looked a little worried. 'Well,' he said at last, 'I suppose I could – though it's not usual, you know. Besides – ' he said, 'it's agony for me. Bad enough granting a wish, but changing one really puts me through it. Still, I must remember that you saved my life – '

So he crossed his great eyes till they clashed together and spun like a single huge Catherine-wheel, and his throat blew up to a great size and he made sounds of magic that were like groans of pain.

'Go on to your Bingo,' he said, when he had finished. 'Your wish is granted.' And turning, he limped slowly to his manhole cover.

The old woman went on to the Bingo hall where her friends were waiting for her. Outside the hall were some shocking-pink posters saying GRAND NATIONWIDE SURPRISE BINGO NIGHT.

When she got into the hall she learned that all the Bingo halls in the land were being linked together by closed-circuit television for this one special night so that the winner could have a grand surprise prize.

How the old woman clutched her Bingo card. How she jumped up and shouted 'Bingo' as her numbers came up. Of course she won the nationwide contest and of course the prize was that villa!

The shopkeeper being cousin to the owner of the Bingo halls had known what the prize was to be and had been telling someone about it on the phone that very morning when the old woman was listening!

They took her straight off in a hired car to see her new home. It was magnificent. All those bedrooms and the swimming pool – the grand furniture, the luxurious kitchen. And besides, there was a cheque-book which meant she wouldn't have to clean the fish-shop floor any more or eat left-overs. She had plenty of money and plenty of time to do as she pleased.

At first she still went to Bingo, but she found that her friends were no longer the same. They either crept and cadged, or they were unfriendly and sarcastic. After a while she stopped going. 'After all,' she said, 'I have my coloured television set, and plenty of comfortable chairs! I can do without friends!' On the whole she was very contented.

And she might have been contented for ever if one evening, when she was watching the television, she hadn't seen a programme about stately homes.

The old woman had never imagined such places existed. Marbled floors and carved panelling, beds with canopies, golden dinner-services, glass-houses full of flowers and fruit, and gardens that stretched for miles with their lakes and waterfalls, and fountains!

'Why hadn't I heard about places like these before I wished?' the silly old woman asked herself.

Without more ado, she sent for a hired car and got herself driven to the corner of the alley. 'You needn't wait for me,' she told the driver.

When he had gone she banged her heel on the manhole cover.

At once it began to move and then fell back with a ringing clatter. The yellow toad crept out. 'Yes?' he said. Then: 'Oh, it's *you*. Don't tell me you don't like the villa?'

'Oh, it's very pleasant,' said the old woman. 'But you see, I didn't know about stately homes when I asked for a villa.'

'Stately homes? And you once lived in a vinegar bottle!' exclaimed the toad, and his great mouth fell open in surprise.

'With fountains and statues and beds with draperies,' said the old woman, 'and pictures and old furniture like on TV.'

'But it can't be done. Not through normal channels,' said the toad in despair. 'It would have to be straight magic and that's worse than the torments of the damned. Why, I might burst with the effort.'

'But I did save your life,' the old woman said.

So the toad sighed and he turned his eyes in so far that they turned the corners and came back the other side and stared towards the opposite side they'd started from, spinning like Catherine-wheels with green sparks flying from them. Steam rose from the toad's yellow forehead and great shrieks tore at his bursting throat.

This time the old woman was lifted up as if by a whirlwind, and spun about and dragged through the air, to be dropped at last on to a fine soft downy feathery dusty bed.

The toad had done real straightforward magic and here she was on a canopied bed in a marbled bedchamber in one of the stateliest homes of England! Even as she puffed and panted to recover from the shock, the door was flung open, and in walked a man dressed as a guide followed by a flock of tourists.

'Oh, I beg your pardon, Your Grace,' he said

to the old woman. 'I thought you were in the family wing.'

Quickly he hurried the staring visitors outside and the old woman climbed off the bed. It was surprisingly dusty and the silk covers were full of tiny slits. Of course, she hadn't known that in a stately home the grand beds were only for show, and the great chairs mustn't be sat on; no one on the TV had mentioned that!

The place was crowded with visitors. Outside more and more coaches were arriving with more and more people. In vain the old woman tried to see her splendid pictures and beautiful statues and enjoy her gardens and everywhere she was jostled and pushed by strangers who told her not to jump the queue. At last she saw a gateway that said PRIVATE, and made her way through to the family quarters where she was really expected to live.

These quarters were comfortable enough, but the rooms were large and draughty, the kitchen old fashioned, and the meal someone had left out for her, which was a salad and a glass of orange-juice wasn't as nice as the left-over fish-and-chips had been.

In fact, the old woman thought it wasn't as cosy as the villa or as convenient as the council flat.

'I didn't know mansions were so hard to live in,' wailed the old woman, as she pushed her way through the afternoon crowds. 'It seems like there can only be one grand place where you're not likely to get this sort of thing, and that's the Palace. They don't have sightseers upsetting Her Majesty.'

Then she began to cackle, and rub her hands together. 'The Palace of course!' She grabbed a passing guide. 'Fetch me a motor-car,' she cried.

After many hours driving through towns and cities, over moors and through valleys, the old woman arrived at last at the town she had come from. Now it was nearly night-time and cold too, but she couldn't wait for morning. Straight to the manhole she went.

'I won't want anything else once I'm set up in London,' she said to herself. Dismissing the car, she tottered to the corner of the alley, and bending down, rapped sharply on the manhole with her knuckles.

Slowly, slowly the cover rose, and fell back

with a hollow clang. Out came a lady toad with a black bow tied round her neck, with seven black-bowed young toads behind her.

'Children,' cried the lady toad. 'This is the ungrateful wretch who killed your poor father!'

The young toads cried out in horror.

'Rubbish, I saved his life,' said the old woman.

'Better he should have died in the dismal drain than perish making impossible magic for a silly old creature like you,' said the lady toad, and she rolled her great eyes, and the seven toad children rolled their great eyes, until they spun like fourteen Catherine-wheels in the gloom.

'Be off to your bottle,' they all cried together.

And back she had to go. To the fish-and-chip-shop yard. There, in the icy yard, she crept about in the darkness, feeling for the glass sides of her old home. It was now so dirty she would never be able to get it properly clean again, its steps had broken away, its door had fallen off and several spiders were now living inside it. It took her a long time to climb up to the bottle-mouth, and crawl in and roll herself up in a corner, but she did it at last, and fell asleep among the cobwebs.

You see, magic wishes are all right if they can be worked out through human agencies. It's straightforward magic that's dangerous. It's not a bad idea to ask someone's advice before wishing.